When A Boss Falls In Love

Tina J

Copyright 2019

Warning:

This book is strictly Urban Fiction and the story is **NOT**

REAL!

Characters will not behave the way you want them to; nor will

they react to situations the way you think they should. Some of

them may be drug addicts, kingpins, savages, thugs, rich, poor,

ho's, sluts, haters, bitter ex-girlfriends or boyfriends, people

from the past and the list can go on and on. That is what Urban

Fiction mostly consists of. If this isn't anything you foresee

yourself interested in, then do yourself a favor and don't read it

because it's only going to piss you off. ☺☺

Also, the book will not end the way you want so please be

advised that the outcome will be based solely on my own

thoughts and ideas. I hope you enjoy this book that y'all made

me write. Thanks so much to my readers, supporters, publisher

and fellow authors and authoress for the support. ☺☺

Author Tina J

More books from me:

The Thug I Chose 1, 2 & 3

A Thin Line Between Me and My Thug 1 & 2

I Got Luv For My Shawty 1 & 2

Kharis and Caleb: A Different Kind of Love 1 & 2

Loving You Is A Battle 1 & 2 & 3

Violet and The Connect 1 & 2 & 3

You Complete Me

Love Will Lead You Back

This Thing Called Love

Are We In This Together 1,2 &3

Shawty Down To Ride For a Boss 1, 2 &3

When A Boss Falls in Love 1, 2 & 3

Let Me Be The One 1 & 2

We Got That Forever Love

Aint No Savage Like The One I Got 1&2

A Queen and A Hustla 1, 2 & 3

Thirsty For A Bad Boy 1&2

Hassan and Serena: An Unforgettable Love 1&2

Caught Up Loving A Beast 1, 2 & 3

A Street King And His Shawty 1 & 2

I Fell For The Wrong Bad Boy 1&2

I Wanna Love You 1 & 2

Addicted to Loving a Boss 1, 2, & 3

I Need That Gangsta Love 1&2

Creepin With The Plug 1 & 2

All Eyes On The Crown 1,2&3

When She's Bad, I'm Badder: Jiao and Dreek, A Crazy

Love Story 1,2&3

Still Luvin A Beast 1&2

Her Man, His Savage 1 & 2

Marco & Rakia: Not Your Ordinary, Hood Kinda Love 1,2

& 3

Feenin For A Real One 1, 2 & 3

A Kingpin's Dynasty 1, 2 & 3

What Kinda Love Is This: Captivating A Boss 1, 2 & 3

Frankie & Lexi: Luvin A Young Beast 1, 2 & 3

A Dope Boys Seduction 1, 2 & 3

My Brother's Keeper 1. 2 & 3

C'Yani & Meek: A Dangerous Hood Love 1, 2 & 3

When A Savage Falls for A Good Girl 1, 2 & 3

Eva & Deray 1 & 2

Blame It On His Gangsta Luv 1 & 2

Meadow

Today was my graduation day and when I say a bitch was happy, I was ecstatic. I went to my closet and pulled out my new Donna Karan wrap around dress with my black pumps by Kate Spade. I hopped in the shower and washed my hair while I was in there. I grabbed the lotion off my dresser and rubbed my hands together before I let it touch my skin. I'm not sure about most people but I hated cold lotion touching me.

After I got dressed, I wasted no time getting to the college. I stepped inside and ran into Khalid who was my on campus friend. He and I became close because we were in school for the same thing. We were both graduating with our Master's Degree in Finance. He was doing it more for his street life and I was doing it to move up in the world and hopefully open my own accounting firm.

He and I never spent time outside of the campus because I wasn't interested in being around his type of crowd plus I kept my heads in the books as well as worked at my dad's company. I never really had time to myself and my sisters call me a cornball. That's why I promised Khalid I would attend some graduation party he was throwing at his house.

"What it do shorty? You're looking sexy as hell." He licked his lips and I rolled my eyes at him. Khalid was fine as hell but I didn't look at him like that. He was maybe five eleven or even six one who knows. His skin was that chocolate but not too dark color and his teeth were white as hell. He had dreads that flowed just past his shoulders and I could tell he stayed in the gym.

Most of the women on campus drooled over him and he loved it. I hated it because we would be studying in the library and I swear it would get packed with chicks and his ass would encourage the flirting. I don't know how many chicks I've gotten into arguments or fights with about him and I not being a couple. I am glad that part of school is over but I am going to miss him.

"Thank you. You're looking handsome too." I told him. He was wearing a pair of slacks and a button up shirt. His shoes looked expensive as hell and I'm sure they were. Khalid had diamonds in his ear and around his neck. I can't count how many different Rolex's he wore so I wasn't shocked to see the new one he sported.

"Let me find out you feeling a nigga Meadow." I cut my eyes at him and we both busted out laughing. He always told me he considered me like his little sister even though I never went out with him past campus but fuck it. I never had to worry about those tired ass niggas that used to try and kick it to me. He would always shut shit down and I appreciated it.

A man was a distraction and I didn't want that when I was in school. Now, that I was graduating, finding me a man was next on my to-do list. Lord, knows pleasuring myself was getting tiring. I needed a man I could wake up next to and hop on his dick or even suck on it.

"Anyway, what's the attire for the party?" I asked and started placing my cap and gown on.

"Whatever you want to wear. You already know I'm going to be on my shit." He said popping his collar. Khalid was definitely a great dresser. Most of the guys couldn't touch him on his worst day.

"Is it ok if I bring my sisters?"

"You know you don't have to ask. Let's go before they call our names and we're not out there." He grabbed my hand and we found the rest of the graduates. After the long ass ceremony I wanted to see Khalid but mad chicks and dudes surrounded him. I went to find my family who I'm sure were already arguing.

You see my mom and dad were no longer together; matter of fact my dad was married but he was not trying to let my mom go. My mom was African American and my dad was Jewish, and as we all know there was no mixing in the Jewish Community.

My dad wasn't the type of Jew that wore those Yarmuoke's or big hats on his head and he damn sure didn't dress like that. My dad was a very handsome man that women of all colors lusted after. He was tall, white with green eyes and reminded you of an older version of Matthew McConaughey and we all know how sexy he is. My mom used to be a model when she was younger so she was tall and thin but not skinny and her body was all that. My father hated that he couldn't be with her the way he wanted but he damn sure wasn't allowing another man to taster her forbidden fruit.

He was married and the wife he chose was more or less just there. They weren't in love at all but he married her just to keep the Jewish community quiet for him having three biracial kids. I believe his wife was seeing someone else too. Shit, she just ought to because my dad lived at our house. That woman didn't even acknowledge us as his kids but we gave zero fucks.

"You better talk that shit to your wife." I heard my mom saying and waving her hand at him. He grabbed her arm and pulled her into him.

"Fuck that paper. You are my wife."

"Yea ok."

"Don't start Karissa." My dad something else in her ear that made her smile. I can only imagine.

"Really. Y'all being nasty at my graduation." I asked and hugged my mom.

"Girl be quiet. You know you're mom has me strung out."

"Yuk dad. Can we go? I'm hungry." My sister Maci said rolling her eyes. My other sister Melina was caking it up on her phone over by the tree. She had just started dating some guy a few months ago that she claimed would be revealed in due time.

Maci and Melina drove with me to dinner where my dad gave me keys to a brand new Audi truck and my mom handed me an envelope with three tickets to Jamaica and five thousand dollars. I knew she wanted me and my sisters to go on a vacation and that was fine but she was bugging if she thought I was splitting the money.

After dinner, my sister's came to my house and that's when I saw the truck. It was cocaine white and inside was red with my initials in the headrest and on the mats.

"You're welcome bitch." Melina said and grabbed her bag out the back. We were all getting dressed at my house.

"For what?" Melina was a bitch sometimes but her and my sister were my ride or die bitches, that's why I didn't have friends. They were all that I needed.

"I helped dad pick this out and told him what you wanted inside." She rolled her eyes and used her key to open my door.

"Thanks sis but you don't always have to be a bitch. You can say it nicely."

"Whatever." She went in one of the bathrooms to shower. I lived in a three-bedroom condo with two bathrooms and one was in my room. It was decorated in red and white throughout my house, which are my favorite colors.

"Fuck her. Let's get ready to turn this party out." Maci said pulling out a tight red dress with some black shoes that buckled around the ankle. The shoes were hot and I was definitely going to borrow them. We weren't rich but my dad owned his accounting business and a few H&R blocks. That's probably why I was into finance the way I was.

I grabbed my Alexander McQueen micro dress with my black lace up sandals to match. She and I both got dressed and went downstairs and found my sister Melina wearing a blue wrap around dress of some kind with shoes to match. The dress color brought the color out in her eyes.

"Here bitches." She handed us shots of Patron. We took a few of them and jumped in my truck. We pulled up to Khalid's house and there were cars everywhere. I text Khalid and told him we were there and he had me bring my car up into the circular driveway. It was only a few other cars parked there.

"It's party time." I told my sisters as we all stepped out.

"Is it just me or is every man out here staring at us?" Maci said closing her door. I saw Khalid coming out and walked towards him.

Khalid

Meadow sent me a text to tell me she couldn't find a parking space and I told her to bring her car up to the driveway. I looked at her like my little sister and I didn't want her walking past all those thirsty ass niggas anyway. Meadow was what us men would call a winner or wife material and most of these niggas here were only looking to fuck. I wasn't about to allow her to fall victim to any of them.

Meadow was high yellow because she was mixed. She had green eyes and stood about five foot five. Her chest wasn't that big and she had an ok body but her ass sat up just enough to make a nigga turn his head when she walked by. However, when she got out of her truck all that changed when I saw her in that tight ass dress. Her body looked like one of those video vixens in the dress she wore. I guess women really do change when they get dressed.

"Hey boo." She came over to me and hugged me. I didn't notice anyone behind her right away because it was so many people coming in and out. I figured they were just off the street.

"Khalid, this is my sister Melina." I spoke to her but she was engaged in a conversation on the phone. She resembled Meadow only she had blue eyes and her outfit brought them out. Another chick was standing next to her fixing her dress.

"This is my sister Maci." When I locked eyes with her I swear I fell in love with her ass immediately. She was a tad bit darker with hazel eyes and a badass body. I licked my lips and stared her up and down. I reached my hand out to shake it and instead kissed the back of her hand. I saw her cheeks turn red as she stood there blushing.

"You are beautiful." I told her and had her step in front of me as I guided them to the back. I admired her from behind and all I thought about was watching her ass jiggle when I hit it from the back. I took them to the back and showed them the table I saved for Meadow. I know this wasn't her type of crowd but I wanted her to be comfortable since she is out of her comfort zone.

"Thank you. I have to say you are very attractive yourself." She said taking a seat. The other sister didn't seem to be interested at all. I saw my boy Gage coming in and told them to make themselves at home. I could see the hate from the other women towards them. I can't front; all three of them were beautiful and should probably be modeling somewhere here or overseas.

"Congratulations bro." Gage said and he and I exchanged hugs. Bruno came in behind him and did the same thing. I noticed him make a face. I turned around and he was looking at the table Meadow was at. There were a few men over there talking to them but I didn't understand why he was mad.

I saw him pull his phone out and start texting. A few seconds later I saw Meadow's sister Melina look down on her phone and excuse herself.

"Hey baby." She said when she came over.

"Baby." Gage and I said at the same time.

"What?" Bruno said with a smirk on his face. The two of them started kissing and we had to turn our heads by the way they went at it.

"Damn, y'all can come up for air." Gage said and we all laughed.

"My bad. This is my girl Melina. I'm sure you met her sisters by now."

"When the hell did you get a girl?" I asked. I was shocked because Bruno never staked claim on a woman. He was more of the hit it and quit it type of guy. Hell we all were. Here he was sitting here telling us he had a girlfriend.

"I asked him not to tell anyone."

"Oh." Was all we could say?

"Yea, my sister isn't the type to deal with men like you. I was trying to find a way to tell her. I had no idea we were coming to this party."

"Well it looks like she knows now because here she comes and she doesn't look happy." I pointed to Meadow who was walking over with a scowl on her face.

"Melina can I talk to you for a minute?" She said. Melina kissed Bruno on the lips and went to see what she wanted.

"Yo, who is that?" Gage said talking about Meadow.

18

"That's Meadow. She and I graduated together."

"Damn, I need to hit that."

"Nah Gage. She ain't that type of chick."

"What you mean? All woman are like that."

"Not that one. She is a hard shell to break. You fuck around and fall in love. Look at this nigga." I pointed to Bruno who was watching the two sisters have a heated discussion.

"Meadow I want you to meet my friend Gage." She spoke and went back to the table.

"I told you."

"That's temporary Khalid. You know how I get." He said and decided to mingle with the crowd. I think he was worried she would shoot him down. I made my way over to Maci and asked her to dance with me. Yea, I had all that out here and the floor was packed with people dancing to "All the way up" by Fat Joe. She and I danced to a few songs.

"Take a walk with me." She nodded her head and followed me. I had a trail in my backyard that led out to a small pond with a bench to sit on. She slid out of her shoe and walked over to the pond and asked if she could put her feet

19

inside. I told her if she planned on killing the fish with her stinking feet.

"My feet don't stink." She whined and smiled.

"Tell me about yourself."

"Well, I'm eighteen and my birthday is a month away." Damn, she was a baby. I mean I'm only twenty-four but still.

"I start college in the fall where I am majoring in business and finance like my sisters and my dad. I love reading and talking long walks. It something about being alone with your thoughts that do something to me. I love Italian subs and eating at the cheesecake factory. And I love to shop." She turned around and smiled.

"Where's your man?"

"I never had one. I was focused on school and trying to get straight A's and become the valedictorian."

"That's good. Did you get it?"

"Ugh yea. I worked my ass off to get that spot and when I give my speech in a month it will be all worth it." Damn, smartness must run in their family.

"What about you? Tell me about yourself."

"I'm twenty four and I just graduated college as you can see." I pointed towards my yard where the people were.

"I'm an only child but Bruno and Gage are my brothers. I don't hang with anyone but them because niggas are jealous and stay plotting on one another." I finished telling her about myself as we sat out there talking for about an hour when the question finally came up. I could tell she wanted to ask sooner but waited.

"Do you have a woman or should I say women?" She stood up and walked back to where I was sitting.

"Not at all. If I did I wouldn't be entertaining another woman. When I love, I love hard and no other woman will get my attention no matter what she did." She gave me the side eye.

"I'm serious. Women always think men don't have a heart but there are some of us out there that can be faithful. Yes, it may be hard with all the temptation but trust me it is possible."

"Wow. I don't think I ever heard a man say when they love, they love hard. What does that actually mean?" I smiled and moved closer to her. I lifted her chin up and turned her to face me.

"If you were my woman I would never cheat on you. As long as you're taking care of home there's not a woman out there who can take your spot. I never allow myself to be placed in a situation where a woman can get close to me or catch me slipping. I also won't allow another woman to approach you with any bullshit. Once you have my heart there's nothing I wouldn't do for you. I would give my life for the woman if I had to."

"Really. That sounds too good to be true." She said sliding her shoes back on.

"I guess you'll never know unless it happens. Let me take you out and see if you are that woman." She moved her hair behind her ear and smiled.

"You want to take me out?"

"Why not?"

"I'm still in high school and I'm a lot younger." I pulled her closer to me and started placing kisses on her neck.

"One, you're graduating next week and if you let me I'll be sitting front and center. And two, it's only a few years." I licked her lips with my tongue.

"Mmmmm. I like that." She said.

"You do huh? Let me see if you like this." I let my tongue enter her mouth and explore inside. The way she kissed had my dick waking up. I stopped and stood her up.

"I think it's time to go find your sisters. But first put your number in my phone." I watched her and realized she how pretty she was. We got to the table and Gage had Meadow smiling from ear to ear. I guess he was right about getting to her but I knew for a fact she wasn't giving up the ass anytime soon.

"Hello everyone." I hated that voice with a passion. I turned around to come face to face with my ex Maribel.

"Why are you here?" I skipped the hello and went in on her.

"I couldn't miss your graduation party." I could see the confusion on Maci's face.

23

"You can go Maribel. I didn't invite you nor do I want you here."

"Oh you acting funny because you have these white girls here." All three of the sisters looked over at her. I've seen Meadow beat a few chicks' asses so I can only imagine how her sisters get down. Maribel had some hands on her too but I wasn't about to allow them to fight.

"What's your name?" I heard Melina ask.

"Why?"

"Because you have no reason to be coming for us when we didn't send for you. If you have a problem with him take it up with him. And yes we may be white chicks from what you see but don't let our yellow complexion fool you."

"What's that supposed to mean?" Maribel was bad but dumb as fuck sometimes.

"It means one of us, if not all of us will beat that ass if you keep running off at the mouth."

"This is my man's house and I can say whatever the fuck I want." Maribel said pissing me off. Maci picked her things up off the table and gave the girls a signal that let them know she was ready to go. The other two stood up and said their goodbyes.

"Oh, look. She's mad. Was that a new contender Khalid?"

"Bye Maribel." I went behind Maci.

"Maci." I called out to her. She rolled her eyes and got in the car. I could understand why she was mad but she didn't give me a chance to explain.

"It's fine Khalid. I'm not mad but I'm also not about to get caught up with an ex that can't let go. I've been around enough people to know an ex that doesn't know how to let go can cause a ton of problems in a relationship and I don't have time for that." She said. I could respect what she was saying but I still wanted to get to know her.

"Maci, let me take you out and explain everything."

"You're begging Khalid." Maribel came up behind me.

"He doesn't have to beg boo. But I see that's exactly what you're doing with your pathetic looking ass. I'll see you around Khalid." Maci said and I smirked. Yea, she was going to be my girl. Any woman that wasn't scared to go against my ex had my vote automatically. After they left I snatched

Maribel's ass up and walked her to her car. She was taking her

ass home. Once I saw her pull off I went back to enjoy my

party.

Gage

I stepped into Khalid's graduation party and I must say there were people everywhere. Not that it was a problem; I just wasn't comfortable not knowing every one. With the type of job we had, our safety was always our main concern. My major concern anyway. Bruno and Khalid had a "if it's my time to go then it is what it is" attitude. Where I wanted to reside on this earth as long as possible. Khalid introduced me to this badass chick named Meadow who had sisters that looked just like her. I admit they were definitely high yellow and looked almost white but I'm not one to discriminate on someone because of their race. Pussy is pussy in my eyes.

At first I thought she would be another notch on my belt until I watched her. I walked around the yard speaking to people but found myself making it back to where she was. At first she was kind of standoffish with me. It took her a good twenty minutes before she found herself enjoying my company.

I found out she graduated with my boy and was opening up her own accounting firm that her and her sisters would run together once they graduated. She hadn't had a man since she got in college and that had a nigga highly interested. That means her pussy was virgin tight and probably feigning for some dick.

She had one her freshman year in college but he cheated on her and it made her lose focus and almost fail out of school. She made a vow not to do anymore dating until she finished.

She and I exchanged numbers as Khalid walked back with her sister. Unfortunately, that went sour when his stupid ass ex Maribel came. She ended up pissing the girls off and they left. I was hoping she didn't bring her ghetto as friend Rylee. I swear that was a stalker at its best. I slept with her a few times but when she started talking about wanting to have a family and all this other mess I cut her off. She was showing up at any clubs we went to.

I had to change my number a few times and I even moved to an undisclosed location because she was showing up unannounced. I guess I wasn't lucky because her stalking ass came up and wrapped her hands around my waist.

"Can I talk to you for a minute?" She asked. I followed her in the kitchen and leaned against the counter with my arms folded.

"What Rylee?"

"Gage why can't we be together?" She asked and pulled my sweats down so fast I couldn't stop her. My dick sprung to life the second she put it in her mouth. I tried to stop her but I didn't try hard enough. I hadn't had any sex in a couple of months because I had been busy working. It's not that I didn't think about it I just didn't want all the complications that came with it like I'm sure this would have when she finished.

"Rylee get up. Shit." I said but as you can tell she didn't listen and allowed me to cum down her throat. Any woman that can let a man that's not hers cum in her mouth it's not girlfriend material at all. It only shows me that she'll do it to anyone. I pulled my pants and her up right before Bruno walked in. He looked at both of us and shook his head laughing.

"Rylee while I appreciate that, you can't keep showing up where I'm at, suck my dick and think we're going to be a couple. It doesn't work like that."

"But I'm only sleeping with you." I gave her the side eye. That was a boldface lie because she was sleeping with a few of my workers.

"Rylee, I'm not going back and forth with you but this is the last time you will do that."

"Yea ok." She said and sashayed her ass out the house. Don't get me wrong, Rylee had some good pussy and her head game was on point too but that psycho shit she did I couldn't get with. The sooner she understood the better.

The party started winding down and I could see the caterers packing up and the maid cleaning up. Khalid was outside saying goodbye to everyone leaving. I looked down at my clock and it was after midnight. The night was still young but after what ole girl just did I was ready to go to sleep. I told my boy I would speak to him later. I was lying in the bed dosing off when I heard my phone going off.

Meadow: *I'm sorry to leave quickly but as you can see the situation was about to turn ugly.* I laughed at the text and how she seems proper but in person you could tell she had hood in her.

Me: *It's ok. I'm glad it didn't have to get physical. I wouldn't want to see your pretty ass fighting already.*

Meadow: *I know right. Anyway, I enjoyed our conversation and I hope you did too.*

Me: *I did.*

She and I texted one another for about an hour when she told me she was going to sleep. I asked her if she wanted company and surprisingly she told me to come over. I know I said I was tired but shit if she was down to see me I was going.

She opened the door wearing a long pajama shirt with some spandex shorts underneath. It wasn't provocative at all. I stepped in her house and everything was red and white all the way down to the rugs. Clearly those were her favorite colors.

"Are you going to stay in here or come lie with me?" I followed her in the room and she had a California King. The shit was comfortable as hell and I felt like I could sleep all day. She got in the bed beside me and before I knew it she was on top of me with her tongue fighting with mine. I could feel myself rising under her.

"Lay back ma." I kissed all over her neck and chest but

I wasn't going downtown. I ran my hands up and down her folds and she was extremely wet. I tasted my fingers and she had a sweet taste but I still wasn't doing it. I stood up and removed my clothes and I saw her smile when she noticed what I was working with. I played around her entrance for a few minutes then forced myself in.

It was just like I imagined. Nice and tight. I could see she was uncomfortable at the beginning but once she was used to me we were matching each other's rhythm.

"Damn ma. This pussy is A1." She wrapped her legs around my back and thrusted under me.

"Gage, it's been so long. I'm about to cum already."

"Let it all out." I told her and felt her wet my dick up so much I thought someone poured water down there.

"Turn over." It took her a few minutes to calm down but she did as I said and threw her ass back. Shorty squeezed her pussy muscles together and was choking the hell out of my dick. I felt my self about to cum and pulled out and released myself on her ass.

I forgot that we didn't use a condom and that was reckless on both of our parts. She hopped up and I heard the water running in her bathroom. She came out with a rag and cleaned me off before using her hands to wake my man back up.

"Shittttt ma." I moaned out when she slid down on it. This chick has some bomb ass pussy and I wasn't sure what I was going to do after today. We just met and here she was giving it to me on the first day. I have to say if I had to wait I probably would've been mad because it was so good.

"Cum for me ma." I said and rubbed her clit. She leaned back and her facial expressions had me about to bust.

"Yes Gage yes." I couldn't hold out any longer and lifted her off me just in time. We both laid there trying to catch our breath. Once again when she got it together we went at it some more. She was like a damn energizer bunny that kept going and going. But I assume a three-year drought will do that to you. The next morning I woke up and it was after ten. I looked over and she was gone. I picked my phone up and saw she left a text.

Meadow: *Thank you so much for last night or should I say this morning; I needed that. It's been a very long time. I am*

33

a carefree and confident woman so if you decide not to deal with me I won't be offended because I know I held it down in the bedroom and I could care less about what you thought of me. Anyway, I had some errands to run. I'm sure you can let yourself out. Until next time."

I found myself chuckling when I read her message. I have never had a woman sleep with me then tell me she didn't care if I called her the next day. I put my clothes on and sent her a message before I left.

Me: *Good morning to you as well. I don't have the right to judge people when I'm not living right myself. But you're right you definitely held it down in the bedroom. I'm glad I was the one you chose to break that drought. You know my number when you're in need."* I hit send and bounced to go home and get dressed. I had my own shit to do.

Maci

I woke up this morning and Melina and Meadow were in the living room watching television. I stayed the night with my sister because my mom and dad stayed having sex and I just wasn't in the mood to listen to it. I went to the bathroom and brushed my teeth and handled the rest of my hygiene. I happened to glance down at the garbage and I saw a damn plan b box in it. I took it out and ran into where they were.

"What the hell is this?" I asked and Melina pointed to Meadow.

"I know damn well you didn't sleep with dude and unprotected at that."

"Girl be quiet. I needed some and he was looking good so yes I fucked him. I didn't have any condoms and you know damn well I'm not having no kids."

"What about diseases?"

"I'm going down to the clinic in an hour damn. I know I was being careless but it was worth it. That nigga sex game is on point and neither of us gave the other foreplay." Melina and I stared at her.

"How the hell was it all that if neither of you went

down on each other?" I asked and they both looked at me.

"Maci, a man doesn't always have to go down on a woman to turn her on. Sometimes a man can give you a kiss that's so passionate down below will start leaking instantly. A man can also find your spot and once he starts messing with it the same thing can happen. Foreplay is not always needed." Melina said and grinned like she was having flashbacks of something her and the guy Bruno does.

"Maci, when you find that right person and he breaks that virginity you're holding on to dear life to, you will understand that once you've had it and stop getting it you'll find yourself needing and wanting it."

"Yea but I'm not going to jump in bed with them the first day." I gave Meadow the side eye.

"Call me what you want but the way we had each other moaning it was worth it." She stood up and grabbed her things.

"See you two later. I'm going to the clinic and then stopping at the store for some condoms."

"Oh my God you're going to sleep with him again." I covered my mouth.

"Ugh hell yea. You'll see Maci. Trust me when the time comes you will see. Love y'all." Melina and I laid around the house most of the day. She wanted to order some movie called Allegiant to watch. I hopped in the shower and put my pajamas on and went back down stairs with a blanket. All three of us used to stay home on the weekends and watch movies on the couch all day. Grant it today was Friday but it was close enough.

"Who is it?" I asked when I heard someone knocking.

"Bruno." I turned and looked at Melina who shrugged her shoulders. I opened the door and he stepped passed me and Khalid was standing behind him looking sexy as hell and all he wore were some sweats and a T-shirt. I stood there lusting after him and he let me.

"Maci are you going to let him in or stare?" I heard Melina yell out behind me. He smiled and came in. My sister and Bruno didn't even stay five seconds before they left us alone. I locked the door and sat back in my spot. Neither of us said anything and pretended to be into the movie. Well I did anyway.

"How are you Maci?" He asked moving closer to me.

"I'm good Khalid. How are you?"

"I'm good now that I'm here with you." I felt the grin creep on my face and could've smacked myself for allowing him to catch it.

"Maci, I came by because I wanted to explain to you the situation with Maribel."

"You don't have to."

"I want to." I turned to face him and let him talk.

"First of all she and I are not together and have not been for the last two years but you were right about one thing."

"What's that?"

"She is an ex that can't let go."

"Ugh you think."

"Maribel and I were together for about three years. She was everything I looked for in a woman or so I thought. I gave her any and everything her heart desired including all my love but she betrayed me." I sat up more because that caught my interest.

"What did she do?"

"I went to jail for something and she must've assumed I would be gone for a long time. Anyway I was only locked up for two weeks because I had the best lawyer and money talks. I had been hearing rumors about her dipping out on me when I was out of town but I refused to believe it. I'm more of the "I need to see it with my own eyes" type of guy."

"Why is that?"

"Sometimes people play on your feelings and try to take something away from you and say shit to try and expedite you doing it."

"Oh ok."

"I came home but no one knew but Bruno and Gage. I was staying with Gage and one day decided to go by her house to see her. Unfortunately I got the shock of my like when I pulled up and the dude came out. They were on the porch kissing and grabbing on each other like they were about to sex one another on the porch. I never said anything and staked out her house for the next few days and sure enough it was the same thing.

Long story short I showed up a month later and she

was talking about she was pregnant. I know for a fact that wasn't my kid because we hadn't been sleeping together prior to me going to jail."

"Oh my God she had a baby on you." He shook his head yes.

"Then why is she bothering you?"

"Because the dude she cheated with can afford her lifestyle and give her all that I did. Plus, she thinks that if she scares away every woman I'm interested in she may have another chance."

"Wow. Do you think she will get one?"

"Not with me. I haven't touched her in over two years no matter how much she's tried." I shook my head because women really did try and hold a man with sex. He and I finished conversing and I must say I enjoyed talking to him. He seemed like a hopeless romantic and wanted to find the perfect woman to start a family with.

My eyes started getting tired and I found myself lying down on his lap. He ran his hand through my hair and it put me straight to sleep. His phone must've been in his pocket because it vibrated under my head waking me up.

"Sorry about that." I smiled and sat up. I apologized for dosing off on him.

"It's all good." I went in the kitchen to get something to drink and when I turned around he was standing right there towering over me. I was a short chick standing at only five foot four and he was at least six foot. He lifted me up on the counter and stood in between my legs.

"Maci, I want to get to know you better." I let my head drop because I felt the same but that ex was going to be a problem.

"I don't know Khalid. I." I was cut short when he placed his hand behind my head and kissed me. I wrapped my hands on his neck. The kiss definitely had me leaking just like my sisters said it would. I felt his hands moving up my legs and instead of stopping him I welcomed it. I let my head fall back as he kissed and sucked on my neck.

I felt his hands sliding up and down my lips and finding my treasure that was getting hard. I may be a virgin but I've pleasured myself many times to know him circling my clit was about to have me bust everywhere.

"Khalid." I moaned out and he went a little faster.

"Cum for me Maci."

"Shit." I felt his fingers find their place inside me and touch something that had my body shaking.

"Come on baby. Give it to me." I bit into his shoulder to try and cover my moans.

"Don't hold out. That's all I want Maci. Are you going to give it to me?" He flicked my clit and put another finger in. I grabbed his neck and sucked on it for dear life as the orgasm ripped through my entire body.

"That was sexy as hell ma." He said and lifted me off the counter and licked his fingers. I tried to stand but my legs were so weak he carried me back to the couch. I heard him go under the counter and when I looked over he was cleaning down the counter with a Clorox bleach wipe. I laid back on the couch ready to go to sleep. I heard him on his phone talking to someone in what sounded like code. He ran upstairs and knocked on my sisters' bedroom door and told Bruno they had to go.

"Are you a virgin Maci?" He asked when he came back in the living room.

"Yes." I said loud and proud.

"Good."

"Good. Why you say that?"

"That means no one has touched you and since you're going to be mine I expect it to stay that way."

"Oh I'm going to be yours?"

"Yup. Matter of fact you're my girl now. If anyone ask you have a man."

"I do."

"Don't play with me. After sampling that on my fingers I don't want another nigga sniffing around you."

"Bye Khalid." He snatched my arm and took me in the bathroom because my sister and Bruno were coming down.

"Do you have a man Maci?" He asked and pulled my shorts down, turned me around and bent me over. I didn't answer and I felt his tongue slide up and down my ass and I almost came off that alone.

"I'm going to ask you again. Maci do you have a man?"

43

I didn't answer not because I didn't want to but I couldn't. He was eating my pussy and ass so good the words wouldn't come out.

"Yes Khalid yes baby. I have a man. Oh shit." I yelled out and in seconds I came all over him. My body would've fallen had he not caught me. I never had my pussy ate but I can say I wanted it again. He sat me down on the toilet and turned on the warm water to wash me up. He cleaned his face off and I gave him some mouthwash to gargle.

"Who's your man Maci?" He asked opening the bathroom door.

"You are."

"That's right. I'll call you in a few." He smacked my ass and followed me out the bathroom. My sister and Bruno were grinning real hard. I hope they didn't hear me.

"Sis are you still a virgin?" I hid behind Khalid and started laughing. He pulled me in front of him, wrapped his arms around my waist and answered for me.

"Yes she is and she's going to stay that way until she's ready." He kissed my neck.

44

"Ok then." Melina said and went out to the car with Bruno.

"Be safe out there Khalid."

"Always." He kissed my lips and got in the car.

****

Khalid and I had been texting one another for the last couple of weeks. Neither of us had time to hook up. With me completing my finals and getting ready for graduation; he was doing his own thing but we made sure to stay in contact over the phone at least. I found myself liking him a lot, which was weird because I never had a boyfriend. Yea, I may have seen some cute ones and kissed them on some dare type of shit but none of them did to me what Khalid did.

"You ready sis." Meadow asked when she came in my room. Today was graduation and I was excited but nervous to stand up in front of all those people. After the ceremony I was grabbing my things when I felt someone grab me from behind. I assumed it was Khalid and smiled. Unfortunately, Khalid was in front of me with a scowl on his face. I turned around and pushed the guy's arms off me. It was my friend Mike who had the biggest crush on me I never gave him the time of day.

"What? You know you like it." He said and sniffed my neck. I couldn't even respond before Khalid had him hemmed up against the wall.

"I'm going to say this to you one time bro. That woman right there belongs to me. I don't ever want to see your hands on her or you sniffing her. Do I make myself clear?" Mike looked scared as hell.

"Yea man damn. I didn't know she had a man."

"Did you ask her?"

"I didn't think I had to. She's never had one. But I get it." Mike held his hands up in surrender and Khalid let him down. I don't know who was more embarrassed Mike or me. Khalid took my hand in his and led me outside to where everyone else was standing.

"I better not see that again."

"Khalid I thought it was you." He stopped and turned to face me.

"I just don't want anyone touching what's mine. I'm very stingy." He said causing me to smile.

"Khalid, I know I've never had a man before but trust me when I say I'm not your ex. I won't cheat on you and you can believe that if I felt like someone was disrespecting me you would know right after I hooked off on them."

"You don't need to fight. That's what I'm here for." He kissed my lips.

"I don't want you caught up in anything. If you're going to get in trouble for anything let it be because I'm about to tear that ass up." He said making me bite my lip. If he can fuck as good as he ate pussy I'm sure I was in trouble. I introduced him to my parents and shockingly both Gage and Bruno were there.

Congratulations were said throughout the group and they even came with us out to eat. My mom told Khalid she hadn't seen me that happy in forever and of course he was cheesing hard as hell.

"You guys seem like a good bunch of men but I'm no fool either." My dad said and me and my sisters put our heads down.

"If my daughters chose you all I ask is that you keep them safe and out if bullshit." We were shocked that was all he said.

"Daddy, Gage and I are just friends." I noticed Gage give her the look of death and I think everyone else did too. It seemed like he cares for her more than she did for him. I found that funny because Khalid told me he was the only one out of the three of them who never caught feelings for a chick. He didn't want to waste his time on a woman that had the ability to hurt him.

After dinner Khalid was talking to my parents and my mom smiled and winked at me. I shook my head and told everyone else goodbye. Melina took my keys and said she was driving my car home. I got in the car with Khalid and we pulled up at the BMW dealership.

"Come get your graduation present."

"Huh? Are they even open?" I asked because it was after eight.

"Get your sexy ass out." He opened the door and helped me step out his car. We walked hand and hand in the shop and some man came out introducing himself as the owner and directed us back to a different area. The cars in here were all

2017. There was a badass black BMW truck that was so nice I didn't want to touch it; afraid I would get my prints on it. Khalid must've noticed me looking through the windows and told me to take a peek inside. Why did I do that? It was so nice I wanted to drive off with it. There were TV's in the back with a navigation system. There was the backup cameras and Sirius radio. The seats were leather with cooling and heated seats. To drive you just turns a knob instead of moving the stick. I popped the trunk to look in it and all these balloons popped out. After they were gone I covered my mouth and turned to look at him.

"Khalid I can't accept all of this." There were bags from Gucci, Prada, Nordstrom, and a few others. I saw a small BVLGARI bag sitting in the back. I opened it and there was an 18k gold mother of pearl bracelet. It was beautiful and I'm sure expensive.

"Khalid this is way too much." He sat down in the trunk and pulled me into him.

"I have it to give you. Can you just enjoy the moment for now?"

"But Khalid." He shushed me by pressing his lips against mine.

"I'm going to spoil you regardless of what you say so get used to it." I shook my head and laughed. He sat there and had me go through each bag in front of him. There was a few pair of shoes, a Celine bag, and clothes; not to mention the damn truck. I thanked him for everything and he had one of the service guys bring my truck around. Once I got the keys I jumped in the ride and peeled out. Khalid called my phone and told me to slow my down and to take my ass home and get ready to go out and celebrate.

Melina

I was getting ready to go out and celebrate my sister Maci graduating from high school. I found myself running to the toilet and releasing more vomit. Yes, I was pregnant; four months to be exact. I didn't want to tell Bruno yet because I refused to allow him to think I was trying to trap him.

I met Bruno seven months ago when I was at college. Meadow, Khalid and I went to the same college but I never met Khalid due to our schedules conflicting but I always seem to run into Bruno. He would pick him up every now and then and I swear he would wait for me. The day he approached I could tell he was nervous which was odd being the type of person he was.

Bruno was a big dude; standing at six foot five and had muscles for days that I loved. I'm not talking about the muscles that are so big the man looks like he can't put them down. I'm talking about the ones that are perfect and have women lusting to be held by them. He was brown skinned with hazel eyes, a goatee and a fade style haircut. My man was fine and the women gawked over him when he stepped out the car.

51

The day we exchanged numbers we've been together ever since. He wanted to bring me around his boys but I wasn't ready for that. Yes, I'm down to hang around anyone but I didn't want Khalid to tell my sister Meadow. She wasn't the type to hang around thug type of dudes that's why she would never hang out with Khalid outside of school. Her ex was a dope boy that cheated on her too many times to count.

The day of the party I was sitting at the table with my sisters when some dudes came up to talk to us. I didn't even notice Bruno walk in but the text he sent let me know I better get my ass up. Bruno was overprotective of me and what we shared together. He always said that men were grimy and didn't care if you had a man.

I told Bruno I loved him last month and I think he became more overprotective. He wants me to move in with him and wants to get married. He hasn't properly proposed but his goals for us were to move in together, get married and then have kids; in that order. Unfortunately, we haven't been using protection and this baby is going to mess up his OCD. Yes, he had a bad case of it. Things had to be done the way he thought it should and if you messed it up he would have a damn fit. I just laugh at him but then he tickles me so bad I end up begging him to stop.

"This outfit is sexy as hell on you Melina. I'm glad you're going to be on my arm." He said walking in the room and pulling me out of my thoughts. I wore a black dress that hugged my curves in all the right places but had a part that scrunched up around the belly area which I needed until I told him.

"Thanks babe." He bent down and laced my shoes up for me and placed kisses up my thigh.

"We're going to be late baby." I tried to move his head that found its way to my clit that was throbbing and begging to be touched. He knew it too and lifted my dress over my hips and took my panties off. The way he sucked made me fall back on the bed and cry out.

"Bruno I'm cumming baby." I let go and listened to him suck and slurp up my juices. He knew I wasn't finished and gave me another one. He stood up and dropped his pants and boxers. I usually always please him orally but right now all I wanted was his dick inside me.

"What do you want baby?" He asked kissing me.

"I need to feel you right now." I didn't even get the last words out before he pushed himself in. I always felt his dick touching my chest no matter what the position.

"Shit Bruno I love you so much."

"I love you too baby. Are you ok?" He started taking slower strokes and stared at me. I had a few tears falling from my eyes.

"Yes. It just feels good and I can't control it." I saw his facial expression and I know he could tell I was lying but didn't say anything. What was supposed to be a quick fuck ended up with him making love to me for over an hour? He carried me in the bathroom and washed us both up. We redressed and headed out to the club.

"Come here Melina." I love the way my name rolled off his tongue. I was standing in front of him at the car. People were walking by speaking to him. He lifted my chin and made me look at him.

"Tell me what's wrong."

"I'm fine."

"Melina, we've been together almost a year and I know when something is bothering you. You can tell me now or later but either way you will."

"Bruno, I'm pregnant."

"WHAT?" I could see people staring at him when he yelled it out. He moved me from in front of him and walked away. That wasn't the reaction I expected but then again I knew he would be mad. I turned around to see if he came back out and when he didn't I called a cab and got dropped off at my moms' house. I sent a text to my sister and told her I wasn't feeling good and couldn't make it. She asked me why wasn't Bruno at home taking care of me and there getting fucked up. I just told her to tell Khalid to make sure he got home safe.

"What are you doing home honey?" My mom came in my room and sat on the bed. Yea, we still had our rooms in my moms' house. She didn't care that Meadow and I moved out she always said we could come back home.

"I told him mommy and he left me standing there after he yelled at me." My mom knew I was pregnant before I did. She said I had a glow around me. She went to the doctors with me and was ecstatic to learn she would be a grandmother.

"Tell me exactly what happened before I send your father out there." My dad may be Jewish but he didn't play when it came to his daughters. He could care less if you were in a drug cartel or not he would come out with his guns blazing over us. My dad's parents were just as happy but my moms, mom told me I was stupid and that I would never be shit because he was a drug dealer and probably had a bunch of babies.

My grandmother on my moms' side was the true definition of a bitch and that's why we didn't fuck with her too much. I think she was jealous that my mom had it all and my aunt Janice was a crack head with three kids she had to take care of.

I told her and she said that I had to give him time and that his OCD was probably fucking with him. She said people with issues like that had to come to grips with things not happening the way they should. Here it is two months later and I haven't seen or heard a peep from Bruno. I called him two days after I told him and he refused my call for weeks and then I tried going to his house but he was never home. I thought about staking it out but being pregnant and always in the bathroom that wasn't happening. Maci asked if I wanted her to ask Khalid where he was but I told her no. I'm not the type to put everyone in my business.

Meadow told me she saw him at Gage's house yesterday and when he saw her all he did was say hi and kept it moving. I was over this childish shit and decided I was going to make him see me and listen. That was if he was even home. I pulled up and his car was there. I got out and knocked on the door. I could've used my key but I didn't feel like it was appropriate being though we hadn't spoken in a couple of months. He opened the door and stood there looking at my stomach and me like we disgusted him.

"What do you want Melina?"

"Is this what it comes down to?"

"Melina you know this is not what I wanted and you." I cut his ass off before he got to say it.

"Don't you dare blame this on me! You could've strapped up. I miss." I caught myself when a woman who was dressed in a short robe showed up behind him. He must not have seen her behind him because he tried to reach out and touch my belly. I backed up and put my hands up. I felt a lone tear slide down my face. I couldn't believe he was already sleeping with someone else.

"What's the matter Melina? Are you in pain?" He had the nerve to ask and sound concerned too.

"Yes but not from the baby." I pointed and he turned around.

"Shit." He cursed under his breath.

"Melina."

"Don't Bruno." I put my hand up.

"So this is the woman that's trying to trap you." She said and my heart broke in two. I knew he felt that way, but to have him discussing that with another woman when I couldn't even get him to say two words to me; felt like he was twisting the knife in my chest.

"That's what you think Bruno." He put his head down in shame.

"Bruno, you know damn well I didn't try to trap you. I don't need a damn thing from you. I thought you loved me."

"I do Melina."

"You couldn't possibly love me if you thought I would try and trap you with a baby that we discussed having eventually."

"If you were supposed to have it later then why are you pregnant now? It looks like a trap to me." The bitch said standing there with her arms folded. I tried to snatch her by the hair and Bruno pushed me back and I almost fell.

"Damn Bruno. You'll push me away to protect her and I'm the one pregnant. Your priorities are all fucked up."

"Melina, I'm not about to let you fight. I didn't mean to make you almost fall so stop being dramatic."

"Dramatic huh? That's not dramatic. This is dramatic." He and the chick stood there while I removed the small 9 mm I had courtesy of him and shot out all his windows and tires to his car. When I was finished he stood there mad as hell and walked up and hemmed me up against the car.

"You're going to pay for that." I chuckled at his dumb ass. I reached in my purse and showed him two thousand dollars in cash. I planned on going shopping for the baby and didn't want to use my credit card so I took cash out the bank. I threw it at him and opened my car door.

"That should cover it." He gave me a crazy look; probably trying to figure out where I got that kind of money. Little did he know my parents were well off and once I turned eighteen I received my trust fund that had five million in it. I didn't need him for shit.

"Like I said before I don't need your ass for shit."

"Where did you get this money from?" He was in my face and I saw ole girl coming out the door and started picking it up.

"None of your fucking business." He grinned and turned back with a snarl on his face.

"You fucking with some other nigga." He had my shirt in his hands.

"Get the fuck off me. You don't need to concern yourself with me any longer. What you need to do is get your woman who is putting the cash in her robe? And you were worried about me trapping you. I suggest you keep your eyes open and leave me the fuck alone. Me and my child will be alright." That shit really pissed him off.

"You will always be my concern."

"Ha. Nigga please." He released his grip and I jumped in my car.

"Bruno lets go. I'm ready to feel that big ass dick in my guts again." I knew she was saying that to be smart and nodded my head. Bruno looked at me and caught me wiping that one tear that slipped out when she said that shit. I was mad at myself for allowing her to get me there.

"Melina."

"No she's right Bruno. I disturbed y'all and she wants it. Go handle your business." I sped off and left him standing there with her. I couldn't do anything but cry. I called Meadow

61

and Maci and had them meet me at Chili's. I was hungry and hurt but I wasn't about to starve either.

Gage

I was sitting at the bar with Bruno and listening to him tell me the dumb shit he did with Melina. I didn't understand how he was with her all this time and thought she tried to trap him. I know they were messing around way before anyone knew but in the short few months' time of knowing her you could tell she was in love with him. He told me how he started fucking his ex to try and get over her but the kicker was what happened when she busted him. I guess she didn't really bust him because he claims they were no longer a couple. Now he was drinking himself to death over losing Melina for good.

"I fucked up Gage. I really thought she was trying to trap me."

"Why would you think that anyway?" He went on to remind me of his ex doing something similar by poking holes in the condom. I had to remind his dumb ass that Melina didn't have to do that because he was a willing participant in fucking her raw.

"I tried to call her and apologize but she got her phone number changed and she even gave her place up to go back home so her parents could help her with the baby. You know how fucked up I feel knowing she didn't have any help and had to go back home. I feel like a loser."

"You are motherfucker and you should. Anyone that has seen you with her knows how much that woman loved you but you let your ex ruin what you could've had with her. When she tossed that money at you that right there alone should've told you she wasn't trying to trap you and instead of running after her you stayed there and fucked your ex who probably got a kick out of the entire thing. Shit, you don't think she came to the door on purpose? Her ass wasn't about to allow another woman get what she couldn't." I know he was thinking about what I said and that's what his ass gets. I was never that type of nigga to bite my tongue for my boys. Hell, if I can't tell you the truth why are we even boys?

He and I continued talking; when I saw this crazy bitch Rylee come in. I thought about getting up and walking away but her ass would follow me so it didn't make a difference. She took a seat on the other side of me and ordered a drink. Maribel was right next to her asking where Khalid was. I didn't have to say anything because he came walking up with Maci who had no care in the world for them sitting there.

"Hey Khalid." Maribel spoke and Maci stood at the bar unfazed, as she should. The one thing I could say about my boy Khalid was he was not a cheater. That shit Maribel was doing to get under Maci's skin didn't appear to affect her at all.

"I see you brought your white girl." Khalid yoked her ass up so fast Bruno and I had to jump off the stool to get him.

"Khalid, get off me." She yelled out and pushed him when we got him to let go. Maci was cracking the hell up which made all of us laugh. Maribel didn't see anything funny and walked up and threw her drink in Maci's face. Khalid tried to get to her but Maci put her hand up.

"Now see if that's funny bitch." Maci took a few napkins off the bar and wiped her face down. She took her earrings and shoes off and in a few seconds had Maribel on the ground beating the brakes off of her. Rylee tried to get in it but Meadow came out of nowhere and tore her ass up. Security came and escorted Rylee and Maribel out. Meadow and Maci stood up without a scratch on them.

65

"Damn, y'all got some hands on you." Bruno said tossing back a shot. I saw the look Maci gave Khalid and I knew it was about to be some shit.

"I'm out Khalid."

"Maci wait."

"Wait for what? Huh? Wait to see her again and have another fight? You told me no woman would ever approach me with bullshit and that's twice already from the same chick. I'm not about to deal with that just to be with you."

"What are you saying Maci because you're not leaving me." We all whipped our heads around. These two have only been together maybe two and a half months and it looks like he was head over heels for her already. Khalid always wore his heart on his sleeve.

"Khalid, school starts for me in two weeks and I can't have this kind of distraction. I've told you that I'm not messing up my education for a man or anyone for that matter. I think we should take a break."

"Go ahead with that shit Maci. If you want to go home because you're mad fine but breaking up with me is not an option. Go sleep that shit off and I'll call you tomorrow."

"It's over Khalid." She asked Meadow to take her home and he tried running after her but we caught him. He had to let her cool off.

"I'll see you later." Meadow whispered in my ear and grabbed my dick.

"You better."

Meadow and I have been sleeping together ever since the first night we met. Yea she bounced the next morning and told me what she did. I respected her even more for getting that pill and tested. She even made me go just in case we ever slipped up. It didn't matter because after we both got our results, we fucked without a condom every time. I wasn't worried about her getting pregnant because she was on the pill and her period just ended.

I didn't want to strap up after feeling her the first time anyway. I followed Khalid home to make sure he actually went there and not to Maci's parents' house. Bruno had to be dropped off too because he was fucked up. I drove around my

block a few times before I pulled in my driveway. I checked

my surroundings no matter where I was. The garage door

opened and I pressed the button and I made sure it closed. I

tossed my keys on the counter and went to clean myself up

before Meadow came. She was the only woman that has ever

been to this house and she had a key. A nigga was catching

feelings for her; what am I saying I already have them for her.

Neither of us ever discusses them because this is only supposed

to be a fuck thing. I'm not sure how much longer I can do this

though.

Meadow

Out of me and my sisters I think I am the only one who is drama free when it comes to the man I'm dealing with. I know we are just sleeping together but at least I don't have to deal with the crap Maci and Melina are. I parked in my parents' driveway and got out with Maci. I went to see my parents and Melina who was getting bigger every day. She signed up to take online classes so she didn't have to wait a semester to finish. I found her in the room lying down watching the TLC channel and they were showing a woman giving birth. I told her what happened with Maci and she shook her head.

"Do you think I did the right thing Meadow?" Maci came in the room and asked me when she got out the shower.

"Maci, if you really like him then no I don't think you did. I understand you were mad but he can't control what that bitch did. You saw how he yoked her dumb ass up when she called you a white girl. I think he is in love with you if you want me to be technical."

"Really. He's never told me that."

"Did you give him the pussy yet?" Melina asked her and we both smirked waiting to see if she did.

"No. I'm scared."

"But you let him eat the cookie that day at my old house." Melina said.

"Yea but that's different."

"How bitch?"

"Because he didn't penetrate me. I've seen that print in his pants and every time I think I'm ready I remember about how big it is and get scared. I know it's going to hurt and I'm not sure if I'll want to do it again after that. Y'all know how I get. When I fell off the bike and broke my wrist I never rode again. Or how about when I jammed my finger trying to play football in gym class. I had mommy get a doctor to excuse me from gym for the rest of the year." She was right. Anytime Maci got hurt on something she wouldn't do it again. There was no try again with her.

"Do you love him?" She shrugged her shoulders and laid in the bed with Melina.

"All I can say is; it's going to hurt not because he's being rough but because he has to break the hymen to get in. But if he's good in bed trust me when I say he will make it feel good in no time."

"But won't I bleed?"

"Yea but not like you have your period. You'll spot but again he won't care because the only thing on his mind will be pleasing you. I can already tell Khalid doesn't ever want to hurt you so I can guarantee that he will take his time and make sure to give you more pleasure than pain." I told her and stood to leave.

"Ugh, where are you going?" Melina asked sitting up to drink some water.

"Oh, I'm going to hop on Gage's dick. See ya." I waved and left them sitting there with their mouths hanging open. Fuck that he wasn't my man but anytime I wanted sex he was the only one who could get it.

I parked my car in the driveway because I didn't feel like opening the garage. I grabbed my overnight bag and went inside to take a shower. I heard him on the phone in his room and decided to use the downstairs bathroom. I turned the water on hot and let it beat down on my body. The showerheads he had always had me in heaven. I washed up and wrapped a towel around me. I stepped out and ran straight into some dude I never saw. I screamed out for Gage and he came running out the room.

"Yo, what the fuck?" He asked the dude who was eye fucking the hell out of me. I backed up in the bathroom and slammed the door. I don't know what Gage said but I could hear him yelling loud as hell. A few minutes later he opened the bathroom door and had me come out. He led me upstairs in his room and shut his bedroom door.

"I'm sorry about that baby." He said kissing my lips, then my neck.

"Who was that? Does he live here with you now?" I was curious because there was never anyone here but us.

"That's my brother and he just came home from jail a week ago and yes I told him he could live here. I told him there would be a key for him under the mat but I forgot it was there.

I hadn't seen him and figured he wasn't going to stay here. I'm sorry I didn't warn you."

"Gage, I don't like the way he looked at me."

"He's harmless baby." I don't care what he said. His brother stared like he wanted to fuck me. I was making sure I never came over unless Gage was here.

"Can I make love to you?" I moved my head back from him when he asked me that. Gage and I only fucked; nothing more; nothing less. When he asked me that I was unsure how to answer him and he didn't wait for me to.

He kissed and sucked on my body from head to toe. I've never had a man suck my toes before and when he did I swear a bitch fell in love. His kisses were getting to close to my treasure and I tried to push him away. Neither of us pleased one another this way so to feel him getting close I was nervous. I always felt that pleasing a man sexually all the way around showed the person you were in love with them. I know some people just eat pussy or suck dick for the hell of it but I thought that was sacred between a man and a woman. Does this mean he was in love with me? The moment his tongue licked my bottom lips my entire body shivered and not from being cold.

"Gage, what are you trying to do to me?" I asked as I gripped the sheets and he sucked my insides out over and over.

"I want to taste that ass next." My eyes popped open and before I could say anything he flipped me over, had my ass spread open and he was making love to it. His fingers were playing with my clit while one was inside me. The feeling took my breath away and I couldn't speak as the orgasm ripped through my body. I shook for a few seconds and my body fell on the bed. He climbed on my back but didn't sit and gave me a back massage as he slid his dick in. He was rubbing my shoulders and stroking at the same time.

"Fuck ma. Your pussy loves my dick." He said as I released again on him.

"Shit Gage." I tooted my ass in the air to feel him go deeper and I think my uterus shifted. He was so deep I found myself running a few times.

"Throw that ass back for me ma." I did what he said. He made love to me in every position possible. He had me moaning, screaming, scratching and I even bit down on him while his strokes went deeper. His dick was so deep I didn't have a choice.

"Just like that Meadow. Fuck yea." He moaned out as I rode him and he came inside me. I was mad but I couldn't say anything at the moment. He always pulled out. He went in his bathroom and came out with a warm rag to wipe us both down. I laid there with my arm over my forehead. This man just made love to me and all I could do was lie here. I felt like he gave me all of him and I was supposed to return the favor. He laid back in the bed and I climbed on top of him and kissed his entire body. I found my favorite part of his body and took him in without gagging. His dick was touching the back of my throat and I played with his balls at the same time.

"Shit Meadow. You sucking the hell out my dick." I sucked and jerked faster and sucked all his cum out like I was dehydrated and needed it to quench my thirst. His body was sensitive to my touch at first. I laid next to him and started dosing off. He pulled the covers over us and wrapped his arms around my waist.

"I love you Meadow." He whispered and I didn't respond. I was shocked because I've listened to him dog women out on the phone and he told me about his psycho friend. He also told me he's never been with a woman long enough to catch feelings.

We've been sleeping together for a few months and gone out a few times but I didn't know it was enough to make him fall for me. I wasn't even sure if I wanted him to. The minute I heard him snoring I snuck out the bed and put my clothes on. I always stayed the night with him. Maybe that's how he caught feelings. I was going crazy with the thoughts in my head. I kissed his lips and grabbed all my things. I opened the door to leave and his creepy ass brother was sitting on the steps smoking a cigarette.

"Put my brother to sleep huh?" He said and had a sneaky grin on his face.

"What?"

"I heard you too in there fucking. You must've thrown it on my brother if he's asleep and you're not."

"What goes on between us is none of your business. And how the hell did you hear? He has a soundproof room for that reason alone."

"My brother may have shut the door but he needs to remember to lock it." He tossed the cigarette on the ground and went to step inside.

"Oh, and you definitely can suck some dick." I covered my mouth and hauled ass. I felt tears coming down and not because I was hurt but because I was mad that another man watched me suck on his brother's dick. I went to my parents' house instead of my own and went straight to the shower in my room. I came out and Maci was on my bed watching TV.

"Why are you here?"

"Gage, told me he loved me." I didn't feel the need to beat around the bush. She sat up smiling.

"So why are you here? Did you say it back?"

"No."

"Why not? You know as well as I that you do."

"I know but what if he just said it because I let him make love to me."

"It's about damn time. You always talking about y'all just fucking now he showed you what he was working with and the first thing you do is run."

"I know Maci. But he caught me off guard with it."

"Meadow you can't keep thinking he's going to be like Bernard. Has he shown you anything other than the fact that he is only thinking about you?"

"No but..."

"But nothing. Take your ass back over there and tell him." I started telling her about his brother and she was just as disgusted about it as I was. I noticed her phone going off only it wasn't from Khalid but Mike.

"Why is Mike texting you?"

"He and I have been texting. We are in some of the same classes." She was attending the local university so my parents could save money on dorm fees and campus food. Trust me they tried to get her to stay on campus but she wasn't hearing it.

"Oh ok. Well I'm going to sleep. I will see you in the morning." I laid there and let my eyes close. My body was so drained I couldn't stay up even if I wanted too.

Days went by and Gage called and text me non-stop but I wouldn't respond. I didn't know what to say to him. He stopped by a few times and I wouldn't open the door but I'm sure he knew I was home. He had Khalid call Maci asking where I was and she told him Jamaica, which I was but came back two weeks ago.

I was still surprised I could stay away from him that long. Does that mean I didn't love him? No I was definitely in love. There wasn't a moment that went by where he wasn't in my thoughts. Every couple I saw kissing, hugging or just walking hand in hand had me in my feelings over him. I guess he got the hint and left me alone because it's been a few days since the last time he called.

****

Melina was going on seven months and wanted to go out to get a new crib for the baby. She had been procrastinating on buying anything but I think it was because she wanted

Bruno to do it. The crazy part is that he tried to get back with her a thousand times and she wouldn't take him back. We stopped in Joe's crab shack because I've been having a seafood fetish lately.

"I want the crab nachos, with the mussels and calamari." I told the waitress ad handed her back the menu.

"Hmmm are you sure you're not pregnant?"

"That's not a lot." I said to Melina.

"Bitch, you never eat that much food." I thought about what she said and I couldn't be. I was on the pill and my period is supposed to start this week. I was stuffing a nacho in my mouth when I felt a presence standing behind me and Melina was grinning. Gage was standing there looking fine as hell. Gage had a cinnamon complexion, he was six foot two with hazel eyes and absolutely no facial hair. The waves in his hair made you seasick and his muscles were showing in his shirt. He had tattoos up and down his entire body.

"Hello ladies." That was all he said and dipped off. I didn't know if I had the right to be mad when I saw this bad bitch go to the table he was at. I pulled my phone out and sent him a text.

    Me: *Oh so now you're seeing someone else. I watched him pick his phone up, smile and shake his head.*

    Gage: *You play too many games. I had to find someone to help me get over you.*

    Me: *Why would you do that?*

    Gage: *Meadow, I know you heard me tell you I love you. I didn't expect you to say it back but I also didn't expect you to leave either. I get it. I'm not going to sweat you or bother you. Enjoy your meal, as will I.* I was pissed knowing dam well I didn't have the right. Fuck it, two can play that game. We finished eating and I couldn't help but stare at him and the woman interact. She seemed to really like him and he leaned over and kissed her lips. That was it. I threw my napkin down and stood up to go over there. I saw him stare at me and smirk.

    Gage: *You didn't want me so don't get mad when you see someone else enjoying my time.* I tossed my phone on the table.

"Don't do it Meadow. If that's what he wants then leave him alone."

"Melina, he's being spiteful. He doesn't give a fuck about her. He's trying t make me mad."

"Then don't let him see you mad." Melina was right. I motioned for the waiter to come over and asked her for the check. It was time to leave and get over this asshole. I could feel him burning a hole in my back. I turned around and gave him the finger and walked out.

Khalid

I wanted to choke the hell out of Maribel that night in the bar. I had just finished talking to Maci about getting her to move in with me. We both knew it was too soon and it was just a thought but we discussed it anyway. Even if Maci wanted to that flew right out the window when Maribel threw the drink on her. I understood why Maci was angry but I can't control what ole girl does. Plus she beat the hell out of her.

When she left that night I gave her a few days to calm down. I tried contacting her on the phone, went to her house and everything for the first two weeks. I can take a hint. I left her alone being though school started for her and I'm sure she was trying to focus. That was another reason I liked her because she was serious about her education.

Her birthday was today. I sent flowers; a card and I put five thousand dollars inside the card. I wasn't worried about the person stealing the money because my aunt owned the flower shop. I sent her a text telling her Happy Birthday and got no response. That was definitely my last time trying to get her to speak to me. She didn't even say thank you for the gifts but I know she got them because when my cousin dropped it off he described her as the one who opened the door.

****

Gage, Bruno and I were going out to the club since we haven't been out together in a minute. I put on an all-black Versace outfit with sneakers to match and made sure not to forget my jewelry. All three of us pulled up at the same time and parked in front. Yea we owned the club and a lot of other shit too. We weren't the type to broadcast our business so no one really knew.

"Y'all niggas ready to turn up?" Bruno said stepping in first. The club was popping with people on the dance floor and at the bar. We spoke to everyone we knew and made our way to VIP. There was always one section left open for us just in case we came.

"Hey Khalid." Some chick named Kima said when I started going up the steps. She was someone I hit off every now and then when I broke up with Maribel. She never had a problem leaving right after sex and didn't expect anything in return. I would hit her off with money anyway.

"Hey Kima." I continued up the steps and sat on one of the couches. It wasn't long before some shit popped off. Two chicks were down there fighting. At first I was going to allow security to handle it until I saw it was Maribel and Maci. I got to where they were and the same dude from graduation had Maci by the arm trying to pull her away.

"Are you ok?" I asked and she rolled her eyes at me. I had enough of her ass and threw her over my shoulder. I let her down when we got to my office. I stood there watching her pout and talk shit about how my ex fucks with her all the time and how leaving me was the best thing she could've done. I let her vent until she plopped down on the couch.

"You finished." She sucked her teeth.

"I can't control what she does and I apologize that she continues to harass you. However, don't come up in here talking shit to me about how you leaving me was the best thing and how some other nigga don't have that kind of drama. You don't want to be with me fine, but that disrespectful shit you talking ends now."

"Khalid I don't know who you think you're talking to."

85

She stood to her feet. She was about to bring a side out of me I only used with people I didn't give a fuck about.

"Listen shorty. I can admit that I wear my heart on my sleeve and I caught feelings too quick for you. But let's get one thing clear though. I'm not any sucka ass nigga you can't talk shit too. That nigga you came with may deal with that but I'm not him. You'll fuck around and get your feelings hurt talking to me like that."

"You know what Khalid maybe he's not a boss like you and your friends are but he doesn't disrespect me or only want to be with me because I'm a virgin." I chuckled. This chick really was funny.

"I think you should go before I hurt your feelings." She stood in front of me and challenged me to say it.

"Maci let's be clear. You're not the only virgin I can sleep with and I'm sure if I went to your high school I can find one over eighteen that would be willing to let me bust it wide open for her. I ate your pussy what, one time right, and I still have never pressured you for sex. You think I can't tell you're scared and nervous? I can tell how tense you get just by me sucking on your breasts. I know you cherish what you have and I would never do anything to make you lose it before you're ready."

"I didn't say that Khalid." I saw her eyes getting glassy.

"Oh but you did. You told me that's all I wanted. Its women out here older than you whom I can fuck the shit out of have suck my dick so good I would keep going back to them. But I was too busy trying to make you my woman. A woman who had no sexual skills whatsoever and would have to be taught how to please me. I was willing to show you just that and had no second thoughts about it.

You had a good man in front of you willing to wait until you were ready to give yourself to him. I didn't even think about anyone else while we were together. I never broke any promise I made you. Yea my ex is bothering you but I can't do anything about it and why should I when you told her we weren't together anyway." She turned her head.

"Yea she told me when I saw her dumb ass at the store and she tried to get with me again. Talking about your girl told me she left you."

"Khalid I just thought."

"Nah, that's the problem you didn't think. All you thought about was my ex and her nonsense. You said fuck what we were building and started running behind dude." I pointed to the guy and he was rubbing all over some chick. I could tell she was in her feelings over it but wouldn't dare say it. That would mean they were together and she wasn't admitting to anything in front of me.

"Look baby girl. I thought mentally you were ready for a nigga like me but clearly I should've left your young ass on the playground."

"Playground."

"Yea the playground. You know where kids like to play games. But let me ask you this." She was at the door ready to leave.

"What?"

"You said all I want is your virginity but how many times has he tried to sleep with you? Matter fact how many times has he asked you to just let him touch it or put the head in." She let her head drop.

"And you chose a nigga who you know only wants that over a man who could care less if you gave it up today or a year from now. Good luck with that." I saw her wiping her eyes.

"Bye Maci." She just stood there.

"How can you talk to me like that Khalid?"

"Easy. I told your ass to leave a while ago because I didn't want to hurt your feelings but you had to be tough so it is what it is."

"Khalid I."

"Get the fuck out now Maci." I opened the door and moved her into the hall so I could lock up. I wasn't about to listen to her cry. Where was all that when I wanted her? She didn't have an ounce of love for me then and I don't have any for her now.

I watched her try and enjoy her night but ole boy was on a roll with the women. I noticed her taking shot after shot and asked Gage to text Meadow to come get her. I knew they weren't messing around anymore but she would definitely see the text and come get her.

Just like I thought about twenty minutes later I saw her sister come in and she stared up at me. I turned my head and continued speaking to Kima who I invited up when I came out the office. I may not be with her anymore but I will protect her as much as I can. The dude she was with didn't even bother to leave with her but you can be sure he will probably leave with one of the chicks on the dance floor. Oh well. That's the man she chose.

Melina

Meadow got a text from Gage saying she needed to pick Maci up. We had just gotten back from Applebee's. Yea it was late night and I was starving. We drove to the club in my dad's brand new Lexus. The car drove smooth as hell. I double-parked while my sister ran in. I was looking around because it was mad people were outside and I always checked my surroundings. I put my head down to scroll on FB and when I put my head up I noticed Bruno had some chick in his face. He wasn't really paying her any mind but the fact he didn't move her bothered be and he wasn't my man. I shook my head and rolled my eyes. Both of my sisters were getting in the car when I heard a knock on the window.

"Let me talk to you for a minute." Bruno said when I rolled the window down. This was the first time we spoke since I went to his house that night I shot his windows out.

"I'm double parked and my dad would kill me if something happened to his car."

"Cut the shit Melina. Move the car and get out."

"For what? You don't have anything to say to me

remember I trapped you."

"I'm trying to be civilized right now but don't think I won't snatch your ass out of there."

"Just see what he wants. You know he will do it." Meadow said.

"Listen to your sister." I moved the car up the street and parked it. I opened the door and the look on his face was priceless. I guess he didn't realize how big I really was.

"What?" I folded my arms and let them rest on my belly.

"You look beautiful pregnant Melina." I rolled my eyes.

"Is that all?" He pulled my hand and had me walk away from the car.

"I'm sorry Melina. You told me you were pregnant and I panicked. You know we had plans to do it differently."

"What about you saying I tried to trap you? And how could you tell that woman those things?" I found myself crying.

"I'm sorry for everything Melina. What can I do to make it up to you?" He wiped my eyes and hugged me. I was going to respond when I heard Meadow yelling at Maci to get back in the car. She was walking towards Khalid and some chick. He opened the door of his car and the woman sat down with a smirk on her face. I took my ass over there to see what was going on.

"Really Khalid."

"Really what Maci? You come up in the club with some nigga and you questioning me on who I take home. You on someone other shit."

"Fuck you Khalid. I was going to allow you to be my first but fuck it I may as well let the another nigga get it."

"Take her drunk ass home." He told us and went to open his car door.

"Nah. Let me get my things I think I just found a winner to give my cookie too. I mean that's what we're doing right Khalid. Taking random people home?" She said and pointed to the chick. I thought he was going to wring her neck. He went behind her after she walked away and Bruno had to go after him.

"Take your ass home Maci." He was pushing her back to where we stood and made her get in the car and put child lock on it. I had to laugh at how comical it was watching her try to get out. I told Bruno I would talk to him later. Khalid pulled alongside of us and wanted her attention. I rolled the window down so she could hear him.

"Maci you did this."

"Fuck you." She yelled out the window.

"No thanks. I got what I need right here." My mouth fell open when he said that.

"Hold on one second." I looked back and she had her phone on speaker. The guy answered.

"Mike I think I'm ready for you to make me feel special and make me a woman." I saw Khalid's face changing.

"Word. Meet me at my house. I'll be there in a few minutes."

"Ok baby. I can't wait." She hit end on the phone.

"I hope you enjoy it. I know this one right here is going to make sure I enjoy myself tonight. Ain't that right?" He asked the chick and moved her closer to kiss her.

"Pull off Melina. I'm over playing this game with him."
I sped off and went to my moms' house. We knew she wasn't

going to sleep with anyone but the shit was funny watching them go back and forth. She hopped out the car crying and ran in the house. Meadow ran in behind her. I grabbed my purse and was locking up my dads' car when Bruno parked behind me.

"Hey." I waddled my ass over to where he was.

"That was crazy huh?"

"You think."

"Where is she?"

"He met us and she got in the car with him." He shook his head while I sent a text to tell Meadow I was outside and not to allow her to come out. After what Khalid did he deserve to think whatever she wanted? I had to tell Bruno that so he would tell his boy.

"Come here." He moved me in front of him, leaned my back to his chest and wrapped his arms around my stomach.

"I miss the hell out of you." He kissed the back of my neck.

"Bruno. Mmmmm." I was trying to fight it but the feeling was so good I couldn't.

95

"I miss you saying my name when I'm eating that pussy."

"Bruno. Stop." His hands were under my shirt. I turned to face him and our tongues met. I heard a car screech behind us and Bruno shook his head and chuckled.

"Where is she?" I glanced in his car and it was empty.

"She's not here. He met us somewhere and she hopped in the car with him. Ugh, where's your date?"

"I was only giving her a ride home because her friend left. You tell her if she slept with him I'm going to kill him and his blood will be on her."

"Hold up. You told her you were about to sleep with the other chick and you kissed her in front of Maci. What did you think she would do?"

"It doesn't matter now. When I find him he's dead." He hopped in his car and sped away with his tires screeching again.

"Is he really going to kill him?"

"We aren't the type of niggas that say things just to say it. Talk is cheap. You better tell dude to go into hiding because he is on a mission."

"You have to tell him not to."

"Hell no. I'm not getting in that unless he asks me. I want you to come home with me."

"Not tonight. I have to call my sister." I told him still trying to play it off.

"Then when?"

"I don't know. I'll call you." I said and went inside. Maci was in my room with Meadow talking about what happened. I told her Khalid showed up and she had a grin on her face.

"Good let his ass stress for once."

"Maci. You have to go find him. You're about to get Mike killed."

"You think he will kill him?"

"Ugh yea. You didn't see him Maci. That man was livid."

"That's what he gets."

"I agree but Mike has nothing to do with that."

"Fine." She snatched up her keys and purse and left. I told her to text us when she found him.

Maci

I was mad as hell that I had to go out looking for this

crazy motherfucker. Why is he mad at me when he's the one who was taken another woman home to satisfy him? I text Mike and told him something came up but not to open his door if anyone came by. He told me he just left and wasn't there anyway. I drove back by the club to see if Khalid's car was there and it wasn't. I just said fuck it and drove to his house. His car was parked and I saw the lights were still on. I shut the car off and blew my breath out. I sent my sister a text to inform them I was here and so was he. I dragged myself to the front door and he snatched it open. His eyes were bloodshot red and he had a bottle of Hennessy in his hand.

"What do you want Maci? Shouldn't you be getting your virginity broken?" He went to shut the door and I managed to slip in before he did. He left me standing there so I locked up and turned the lights off. I went upstairs and he was on the edge of the bed with his head in his hands.

"Maci, I'm going to ask you one more time. What are you doing here?"

"I came to make sure you were not out trying to kill Mike."

"Oh, you're worried about that nigga?" He chuckled and went in the bathroom. I heard the shower start and sat there. I wasn't going in there. I've seen men naked on television but not up close. He probably didn't want me in there anyway.

"Maci, come here." I guess he did. I stepped in the bathroom and I could see his silhouette though the glass that was full of steam."

"What's up Khalid?"

"Can you pass me a towel?" He asked and I waited for him to shut the water off. I handed him the towel over the shower door. I could see him drying off and then wrap the towel around him. He opened it and all I wanted to do was jump on him but I was scared as hell. He took my hand and had me walk in the room with him.

"Maci, did you lose your virginity?"

"No Khalid." He lifted my chin and kissed my lips. I loved the way his tongue and mine played together. I scooted back on the bed and he climbed in top of me. I felt his manhood rubbing against my pelvis and it was feeling good. He kissed my neck and stopped. I wrapped my arms around his neck to pull him closer.

"Khalid, I want you to be my first." He stood up and slid his basketball shorts on under his towel.

"I don't want it."

"Huh?"

"You heard me. I don't want it."

"If you didn't want it then why did you threaten to kill him if he got it?"

"I didn't want him to have it. Maci, what happened tonight doesn't change anything. I wouldn't feel right taking it and we're not together and you don't love me."

"What does that have to do with anything? You were going to take it before."

"I was because I knew we would be in love by then but you broke up with me and then tonight you dangled your virginity in my face as if it was a toy and didn't mean anything to you. Maci, you're losing yourself and it's not because of me. What's going on with you?" I just started crying. He was right. I was losing myself. All this was out of my character. I didn't say anything and got up. I went back downstairs and laid on the couch even though I wanted to leave. It was way too late to drive home. My eyes were getting heavy and I couldn't keep them open anymore.

I kept hearing a noise in my ear while slept. I turned over and realized I was in Khalid's bed only he wasn't there. I picked my phone up and glanced at the time. It was after ten in the morning and my head was killing me. I picked my phone and keys up and went to leave. I still didn't see Khalid anywhere. Last night made me realize that I don't need any man in my life and that I had to get back to focusing. I sent him a text telling him I locked the bottom lock and I would see him when I see him.

"Hey you two." I said when he walked in Melina's room.

"What's up? You want to go with me to the Olive Garden?" Meadow asked and Melina looked at me.

"Sure. Why are you looking at her like that Melina?"

"I keep telling the bitch she pregnant."

"You are?"

"Hell no." My period will be here this week." Meadow

said.

"Maci, she's been saying that shit for two weeks now. Do me a favor when y'all leave the olive garden, pick up a test so her ass can take it."

Meadow and I went out to eat and I told her everything that happened. She said I should be happy Khalid didn't take advantage of me. I wasn't feeling her being on his side. She and I were leaving and there he was walking in with the chick from last night. He spoke and kept it moving. I can't lie I was fuming but I held my head up high.

"You ok?" She asked me.

"Yea. I'm good." I went in my room when I got home. I laid around most of the day until it was time for me to go out. I looked through my closet to find an outfit to party in. I was over these niggas for real. Meadow said she would come out with me but she wasn't staying out late. I just wanted to have a few drinks. I took another shower and put on some skinny jeans, a sweater and ankle boots. Nothing spectacular for a bar.

"What can I get for you?" The bartender asked.

"I'll have two shots of Patron and a Corona." I told him

and Meadow ordered a jolly rancher. I guess she wasn't

pregnant if she was out drinking. An hour later and a few more

jello shots later I was feeling it. My song On the Run by Jay Z

and Beyoncé came on and I went out to dance.

I don't care if we on the run, baby long as I'm next to

you

And if loving you is a crime, tell me why do I bring out

the best in you,

I hear sirens when we make love, loud as hell, but they

don't know,

They're nowhere near us. I will hold your heart a gun;

I don't care if they come.

They can take me, without you I have nothing to lose.

I felt a pair of hands behind me dancing and didn't

bother to turn around. I let him grind all over me song after

song. I was in a zone and gave zero fucks at this point. After a

few more songs I figured I would turn around to see who I was

dancing with and looked right in the eyes of Khalid. I rolled

my eyes and went to walk away. He snatched my arm and

pulled me back to him.

"Get in my car." I had to make sure I wasn't hearing things.

"Here are the keys. I'll be there in a few minutes." I saw Meadow getting up to leave.

"You were just going to leave me?"

"No bitch but he said you were going home with him." She kissed my cheek and walked me to his car. I got in on the passenger side and let my seat go back. I few minutes later Khalid was driving. I don't even know when we got here. I just felt him carrying me in the house. I was lying down when I could feel him taking my clothes off.

"Khalid are you going to make love to me?"

"Good night Maci. I'm just putting a t shirt on you so you can sleep comfortable." I laid back with my arms folded and my lips poked out. I could hear him snickering. I jumped up and ran to the bathroom. I looked at myself in the mirror and laughed. My hair was all over the place and my lipstick was faded. No wonder he didn't want me. I grabbed a washcloth and turned the shower on. I hopped in and Khalid stood there and took the washcloth from me. He washed my entire body and carried me back to bed.

"Good night Khalid." I rolled over and a few minutes later I felt him rubbing lotion on my body. He was gentle going in and out my legs and up and down my back and front. I caught myself let out a soft moan and I think he did too because he laughed.

"Make love to me Khalid. Please." I sat up and pressed my lips to his and parted them with my tongue.

"Maci. You've been drinking and I'm sure it's making you horny."

"Khalid fuck this." I lifted my shirt over my head and pushed him back on the bed. I felt his hands roam up and down my back and ass.

"Move up Maci." I wasn't sure what he meant and sat up.

"Move up where?" He laughed and had me scoot up until my pussy was on his face. I was about to say something until I felt his tongue go up and down and then he sucked on my clit. I was in pure heaven. I thought him doing it from the back was the bomb but this right here was better.

"Khalid I'm cumming." I shook and fell back on the bed out of breath. He sat up and pulled me to the edge and dove back in. I had my hands wrapped in his dreads and my hips grinded on his face.

"Yea Maci. Fuck my face baby." He lifted up to say and stuck his finger in. I arched my back and the juices came rushing out.

"One more Maci. That clit is hard again." He latched on and I screamed so loud I probably woke the neighbors. He stood up and kissed my lips.

"Go to sleep Maci." He must've thought I was playing. I jumped up off the bed and pushed him against the wall.

"Maci, you're tripping." I pulled his pants down and his dick popped me right in the face. It was huge and I was scared to death. He went to pull me up and even though I should've gotten up I didn't. I opened my mouth and sucked on the tip and then licked up and down the side. I was trying to remember all the women I saw on porn sites and how they did it. I did remember to spit though. It took me a few minutes but I got in a zone and I was sucking him off like a pro.

"Damn Maci. Fuck." He had his hand on my head and I looked up to see him watching me. I suctioned my cheeks to make more of a vacuum feeling and that's when his body started stiffening up.

"Get up Maci. I'm about to cum." He was holding on to the dresser with one hand.

"Let me taste you Khalid." I looked up and he was smiling.

"Fuck baby. Shittttt." He moaned out and the warm juices he released hit my throat and I accepted all of it. Who knew I would enjoy giving head? I stood up and went to the bathroom to rinse my mouth out. I came out and he was in the same spot.

"I'm ready Khalid." He came over to where I was and kissed all over me.

"Maci, are you sure?"

"Yes baby. Put it in." He put the head in and I thought he was ripping my insides out, and it got worse the more he went in. He put his tongue in my mouth and entered me in one push. I yelled out and my nails dug in his back. He went slow and kissed me over and over. My body started relaxing and I found myself moving with him.

"It feels good Khalid. Oh shit, it feels good." He didn't say anything and lifted my legs up and dug deeper.

"Maci, I swear nobody else better have this. This is all mine."

"You sure you still want it? Fuck." I asked and came at the same time.

"Maci, you've always been mine. Turn over." I did what he said and I'll be damn if this position wasn't just as good.

"I want you to teach me how to ride you Khalid. Teach me how to fuck the shit out of you." We had sex in every position more than once.

"Ride it Maci." I stood on my feet like he told me and had him moaning out my name.

"I'm about to cum Maci."

"Me too Khalid. Fuck. I love you." I couldn't believe I said it.

"I love you too baby. I never stopped. Ahhh shittttt."

He let all his kids swim in my stomach. I laid on his chest.

"I meant what I said Khalid. I love you."

"I love you too Maci."

****

I can't lie; last night was a night to remember. After we had sex he started a bath for me so I wouldn't be too sore but it only helped when I was in the tub. Once I got out it still hurt. I can say that it was definitely worth it and I wanted some more. I woke up to his phone ringing and picked it up.

"Hello."

"Can I speak to Khalid?" She was nasty but I wasn't about to argue with this chick when he was lying up under me.

"Khalid." I nudged him a little.

"Yea baby." He said groggily.

"There's a woman on your phone asking for you."

"Did she say what her name was?" I asked her and she got nasty again.

"Here, I'm not about to allow her to keep getting nasty with me." he took the phone from me and blacked out on whoever it was for getting smart with his woman. I don't recall him asking me to be his chick but I wasn't complaining either.

"Baby, she wants you." He handed me back the phone. I gave him this crazy ass look.

"Hello."

"I apologize for getting smart with you. I didn't realize you were his woman."

"Ok I guess. Why are you contacting him anyway?"

"Khalid and I used to mess around. I thought he wanted to make me his chick because he brought me out to eat yesterday and then I didn't hear from him again."

"Did you sleep with him?"

"No he wouldn't let me and I tried." I smiled and told her goodbye. To know he waited for me had my pussy sore but ready to show him my appreciation. He was in the shower and shockingly I got in with him. I thought about him entering me and changed my mind when I looked down and remembered how big he was. I'd rather give him head until I got used to him. I dropped down and he moved back against the wall for support.

111

"Suck that shit Maci." I don't know why but it turned me on when he spoke like that. I went harder sucking it and he pulled me up after he came. I wasn't ready for what came next and that was him sucking and eating me out from the back again. This man had me cumming for days.

"Baby, I'm going back to sleep." I told him and got in bed naked. I tossed the covers over me and was out. Good dick will make you do that I guess. I was in a deep sleep when I heard Meadow in my ear. I thought I was dreaming at first until her ass pulled the covers back and smacked me on my ass.

"Hey that's my ass to smack. Keep your hands off." I heard Khalid say.

"Oh shit bitch. You finally gave him the cookie. He beat it, beat it up." She was singing that beat the pussy up song. I sucked my teeth and put the covers back on me.

"How was it?"

"Really. Khalid is right there." He was sitting at the edge of the bed cracking up.

"Who cares? It must've been real good if you're in this bitch sleep and not answering my calls."

"I didn't hear my phone and it was real good." I said when I saw him walk out the room.

"Ok. Tell me something." You know my sex life is back to being nonexistence so I need to live vicariously through you."

"Sis, he made love to me all night. Once he made me cum the first time my body wouldn't stop yearning for his touch. I needed to feel him inside me and if he could've slept in it I damn sure would've let him. And I can't even explain the mind-blowing orgasms. Meadow I didn't know it was this good."

"Hell yea it is. Especially if the nigga loves you. The chemistry is way different when feelings are involved."

"Do you love him?"

"With all my heart Meadow. I may be young but I don't see myself without him. You already saw how miserable I was when we weren't together. I don't want to feel like that ever again."

"And you won't because you're moving in." Meadow and I glanced over at him and he was standing there putting on a t-shirt. He came to where I was and handed me his black card and told me to go shopping for everything I need. All my school things will be brought over later and he had some architect guy coming to make one of the extra rooms an office so I can do my homework in there.

"Khalid, this is too much."

"What did I tell you when we first met Maci?"

"That when you love, you love hard and whoever the woman is you will give her the world." I wiped my tears.

"And you are her."

"I am?"

"I love you just as much as you love me. There's no need to go through any more stress when we can be together. Now get your sexy ass up and go do some damage with your pregnant ass sister."

"Who told you that?" Meadow said and looked at me.

"No one. Your stomach is poking out. Does my boy know?"

"No and don't tell him. I will tell him when the time is right."

114

"That's your shit but you see how I am over her. That nigga is the same way over you. The time to tell him is now and not before someone beats you to it."

"He doesn't feel the same."

"What is up with you sisters? You have three boss ass niggas in love with y'all but yet none of you can stop being stubborn long enough to accept it. You're too busy thinking it's not real. Take that wall down and love that man. He told me you left when he told you how he felt. Did you stop and think about how he felt? Think about that. Maci, I have to go. I'll call you later." He kissed my lips and left.

"You think I should tell Gage?"

"I think you should before someone else steals his heart from him. I'm taking a quick shower and then we can go."

"Make sure you wash all that cum off. Don't nobody want to be smelling that while we're shopping. Yes, I said we because I'm putting shit on the counter." I busted out laughing and handled my business. I was living high right now and refused to allow anyone to bring me down.

Meadow

I stared at the prescription for prenatal vitamins that my gynecologist handed me and felt a tear drop. That and the ultrasound picture had me at a loss for words. All this time I stayed focused and the first time I hop on some dick I pop up pregnant. I can't get rid of it because my parents would kill me and I know damn well Gage will. He's mentioned on many occasions that he wanted to have a family and looking for the right woman. I stood up and grabbed my things to leave. My car seemed far away as I dragged myself to it.

I know a child is a blessing but right now I had so much going on. I was having a grand opening this Saturday for my new accounting firm. Yes a bitch is working. People may think hearing our story that we were just running behind these niggas but we are handling business. Anyway, my sisters and I own it together but since they're still in school I will be running it alone. They will be there to help out though.

"Stay away from my man bitch." I heard someone yell out while I was at the red light. Now hearing a woman say bitch had my ears wide open. I looked around and no one was there.

"I'm over here dumb bitch." Ok she said it twice. I pulled my car over and got out to see what she was talking about. I see some chick standing there looking ghetto as hell. Her hair was purple. Yes I said purple. She had a pretty face and her body was on the decent side. Her clothes didn't appear to be too expensive but I don't judge.

"Excuse me. Are you talking to me?" I asked still

approaching her.

"There was no one at the light but you." She pointed around to say we were the only two out there.

"Who are you?" She smirked and put the cigarette out she was smoking and threw it by my foot. Oh yea she was testing me.

"My name is Rylee and Gage is my man." I threw my head back laughing.

"Are you serious? Gage and I haven't been together in about a month. Wait, how do you even know who I am?"

"You're asking too many questions. Stop being nosy."

"Oh shit really. You approach me about some guy I was only sleeping with and tell me I'm being nosy. Do me a favor and don't say anything else to me." I went back to my car and listened to her tell me to leave her man alone. Gage must be sleeping with mad people because that is not the woman from Joe's Crab Shack.

I stopped by the pharmacy to pick up the vitamins and a few magazines. I ran across a few baby ones that caught my eye and picked them up too. I was looking down when I ran smack dab into someone's chest.

"I'm sorry." I looked up and it was Gage's creepy ass brother. He licked his lips and folded his arms in front of him. I tried to move past him but he kept blocking my way.

"Did you get what you needed?" I heard Gage's voice in the store.

"Yup found it." He smiled and I went in the other direction.

"Meadow Woods your prescription is ready." I heard over the intercom. A bitch was mad as hell they blasted me in the store like that. What if I had a disease or something? I was making sure I addressed the pharmacist. I made my way to the back and there he stood glancing down on his phone. He wore a pair of black sweats, a V-neck t-shirt and some fresh Jordan's. His hair was freshly cut and the way he licked his lips made me walk with my legs tight. This man did something to me everything time he was in my presence.

"Here's your prescription." I went to pay and the guy told me it was paid for.

"I'm not going to ask you what that's for. Just tell me if

I need to be checked out." He said calmly. I think I was offended. But did I have the right? I did sleep with him the first night. No we both got checked and I was exclusive to him.

"I'm not even going to entertain that. You know who I am and what I'm about. If you feel like that's something you need to do then be my guest. I snatched my bag and walked to the front to pay for the rest of my things.

"Why do you have baby magazines?"

"You do remember my sister is pregnant. Why are you all in my stuff anyway?"

"One, I'm not all up in your stuff because if I were you would be screaming and we both know it." The cashier was some young teenager and when she heard him say that she gasped and covered her mouth.

"Bye Gage."

"No one is going to make love to you the way I do." He said being smart. The cashier dropped my card when he said that.

"You make me sick."

"Bye Meadow." He swirled his tongue around in his

120

mouth for me to see and my clit jumped at least ten times. I took my card back and walked to my truck. There was a text on my phone.

"You better be at my house by nine. Don't make me come looking for you." I grinned and took my ass home. He was crazy as hell if he thought I was going over there. I went home and cleaned my house then laid around. It was after eight and another message came through on my phone.

"Bring your ass outside." I put my phone down and laid there. Who did he think he was? My phone went off again.

"NOW!" I heard banging on my door and jumped.

"What Gage?" He lifted me over his arm and put me in his car.

"Get out!" I folded my arms on my chest and refused to get out. He came and took me out.

"Why are you acting up?" He asked kissing on my neck and lifting my shirt over my head. Yea, I could've stopped him but I didn't. He unstrapped my bra and my breast spilled out. He attacked both of them gently but rough just the way I liked it. He sat me on the dresser and devoured my pussy as if I was a steak.

"Damn Meadow that pussy won't stop cumming for me." He said and went back to finish.

"Did you miss me?" I asked and walked over to where he was sitting.

"A whole lot. Shittttt." He moaned out while I sucked him off. His cum tasted so good I got him back up just to do it again. This time he was begging me to stop. He climbed on top of me and stroked himself to get up and entered me forcefully.

"I love you Meadow." I opened my eyes and he was smiling down on me. I hated that this kid made me a crybaby already. I felt the tear come down my face. He lifted my legs on his shoulder and went deeper.

"Do you love me Meadow?" I couldn't answer him because the spot he hit made me lose my breath. He stopped and pulled out a little then rammed himself back in.

"Fuck Gage."

"Meadow don't make me ask you again." He hit that spot again.

"Yes baby yes." I screamed out as I came hard.

"Yes what? Why are you crying?"

"It feels so good." He flipped me over so I could get on top. I slid down as much as I could without hurting myself. They say a woman can't take it the same when she's pregnant. Since he doesn't know yet I have to roll with the punches. I went up and down and he was moaning almost as loud as I was. He pumped harder under me and played with my clit. The feeling was overtaking me.

"Gage. Oh My God. What are you doing to me?" He sat up and held me tighter as he continued pumping.

"I love you Gage. Shit, I love you so much. Yeeeeesssssssss." He grabbed my face and kissed me aggressively.

"Damn I love hearing you say it. Say it again." He said and had me turn around to ride him backwards.

"I love you Gage. Please don't hurt me." I felt his hand massaging my clit. He turned my face to kiss him when I stopped moving.

"Keep going Meadow."

"I heard something." I jumped off him and pulled the

covers to my chest.

"Baby what's wrong?" I pointed to the door.

"Gage there was someone at the door."

"There's no one here but us." He put his boxers on and went out the room. He came back a few minutes later saying no one was there but I know what I saw. I bet it was his perverted ass brother. I made him lock the door before we finished. I wasn't into like I was previously and he knew it.

"Baby its ok. I would never allow anyone to watch us have sex."

"I know. But I'm telling you someone was standing there."

"Meadow the only other person staying here is my brother and he's not here."

"Are you sure he's not here?"

"I went by his room and it's locked." I don't care what he said I still had that feeling. We took a shower and I fell asleep under him. I didn't leave any space in between us because I was so scared. The next morning I woke up before him and handled my hygiene. I took a peek out the window and his brothers' car wasn't in the driveway. I put on Gage's t-shirt and went down to make breakfast. I cooked him bacon, eggs, toast and grits. I poured him orange juice and had his plate in my hand.

"Good morning. Did you make me one?" His voice sent chills down my spine and not good ones.

"I didn't know you were here." I turned around and that's when I noticed the resemblance. He wasn't as handsome as Gage but his build, complexion and hair was the same. I tried to remain calm but the way he was staring was creeping the hell out of me. He stared me up and down and licked his lips. I was kicking myself because all I had on was a t-shirt. No bra or panties.

"Why would you think that? I live here."

"My bad." I backed into Gage's door. I was getting ready to turn the knob.

"You're making me jealous when you're fucking my brother."

"What did you just say?" He walked up close enough to whisper in my ear.

I really enjoyed the way you suck dick but watching you riding it was even better."

"You were standing there."

"I sure was and I must say I came hard in my hand." I smacked him across the face. He just walked away laughing. I shut Gage's door and locked it. He was coming out the bathroom with a toothbrush in his mouth. I put his food down and started putting my clothes on. I had to get out of this house.

"Baby, what's wrong? You're shaking."

"I have some things to do that's all."

"Meadow, tell me what's wrong?"

"Nothing baby. I'm just stressed out a little. I'll see you later ok." I kissed him and ran out the house. I started my car and looked up to find that motherfucker standing in his window sticking his tongue between his two fingers. There's no way in hell I'm coming back to this house. I don't give a fuck what Gage says. I drove to my house so fast and ran to the shower. I scrubbed myself until my body started turning red. I'm not sure why because he didn't touch me but to know he watched me and got off on it made me feel like I was. Now I know what it felt like when that lady from ESPN said someone was watching her and felt violated. It may not be a physical rape but a mental rape is just as bad. I dried off and put lotion on. I heard banging on the door and sat there. I heard my phone go off.

Maci: *Open the door sis; it's me and Melina.* I got up off the bed slowly and made my way downstairs.

"What happened?" Maci said and Melina started waddling her big ass around the house.

"Nothing why?"

"Gage called Khalid and Bruno and said for us to check on you because you left out upset and shaking this morning." I plopped down on the couch and started crying.

"Who do I need to shoot?" Melina said taking a seat next to me. I told them what happened both times and they were in shock. Maci and Melina both said I should tell him but I didn't want to cause a beef between them. I made both of them promise not to tell Khalid and Bruno. They stayed with me for the rest of the night. I woke up the next day in my bed and Gage was lying with me.

"You good baby." He said and moved me closer to him.

"Yea. You hungry."

"Yes, but not for food."

"You are so nasty. I want to talk to you about something." I wasn't going to discuss his brother but I did feel the need to mention the baby. I was cooking when I heard him going off on someone upstairs. I turned the music up on my phone to block him out.

"Everything ok?" Now it was my turn to ask.

"Yea but I have to go."

"Gage, I really need to talk to you about something."

"Ok. You can tell me after dinner tonight with my mom."

"Huh?"

"Don't huh me. We're having dinner with my mom. I have to introduce her to my woman and possible wife." I just nodded my head.

The rest of the day I stayed in the house going over the food and seating arrangements I wanted for the grand opening. Yea I had a lot of different firms coming as well as sponsors. I glanced at the clock and noticed it was after six and Gage said he would be there by seven. After I got myself together he sent me a message saying he was outside. We drove to his moms' house talking about bullshit. The first car I noticed was his brother.

"Don't worry baby. My mom is going to love you." He pecked my lips.

"It's not your mom I'm worried about." I mumbled when he got out the car. The minute we stepped inside I heard someone suck their teeth. I turned my head and it was his mother.

"Hey ma. This is Meadow, Meadow this is my mom." I smiled and spoke while she rolled her eyes and talked shit.

"Meadow. What kind of name is that and is she white?"

"Yo ma. I'm telling you right now you start some shit and I'm out. Who the fuck cares if she's white or not? But if you must know she's mixed." I didn't think he should've told her that.

"I'm just saying she's very light." She rolled her eyes again at me. His brother came in and I saw the look he gave his mom and she nodded.

"Gage, can you run to the store and get me some more sugar?" I was right behind him.

"No she can stay. That will give me time to get to know her." Gage looked at me and I shook my head no.

"Don't be like that honey. I know I came off wrong but let's talk." She grabbed my hand and told me to sit at the table. Gage smiled and walked out. Once his car pulled off she didn't say two words to me. I sat there texting my sisters letting them know I may need one of them to come get me. I felt my baby sitting on my bladder and as bad as I wanted to wait I couldn't hold it any longer. I walked in the living room and asked his mom where the bathroom was. I locked the door and handled my business. I opened the door and Jesse, Gage's brother, who I just found out was his name was standing there. I tried to move past him and he pushed me back in and started sniffing my neck.

"Get off me." I pushed him back and he laughed. I looked out the door and his mom smirked and left. What the hell is wrong with this family?"

"You know you want it. That's why you haven't told my brother." His hands were all over my body.

"I haven't told him because he will kill you."

"Yea right. He'll believe me over you." Jesse please leave me alone. Before I could stop him his hands were in my pants and his fingers were in my pussy. He wasn't gentle and his nails were scratching the hell out of me. I started screaming out as he kept going in and out. I used all my might to try and move his hand but he was too strong.

"Get off me." This nigga pulled his dick out and started jerking off at the same time.

"Shit, your pussy wet. Cum for me Meadow."

"Please stop." I was crying so hard I didn't realize he came until he took his hand out my pants.

"And you taste good. I see why my brother is strung out." He put his dick back in his pants.

"Jesse he's back." I couldn't believe I heard his mom say that. This bitch was in on it.

"If you say anything I will kill you. I can't wait to have you sitting on my face." He said and walked out. I sent Maci a

131

text and told her to please come get me. I was done with Gage and this family. I know it's not his fault but I can't be around this. Who the hell finger rapes their brothers' woman? A crazy motherfucker that's who.

Gage

My mom pissed me off coming at Meadow for no reason. Then she had the nerve to try and make it up by having me stay there to talk to her. I tried to stay at the store a little longer to give them time but I started missing Meadow. I don't know what she did but my ass was head over heels in love with her. Who knew a Boss nigga could fall in love? I never thought that shit was possible. Most bitches wanted and tried to get me for all I had but I was always a step ahead. I turned the car off and opened my moms' door. Jesse was on the couch and my mom was in the kitchen pouring herself some soda. I looked around for my girl when I didn't see her. I saw the bathroom door was closed and assumed she was in there.

"Meadow are you ok?" I asked knocking on the door. She unlocked the door and her face was red and puffy and she was hysterical crying. She pushed past me and went straight outside. I stopped in the living room where both my mom and brother were now sitting and asked them what happened. Neither one seemed to have a clue. I ran outside and Meadow was standing there.

"Baby, what is going on?"

"Nothing Gage. I just want to go home."

"Fine but you're coming home with me."

"I don't want to go to your house."

"I don't care what you want. You're coming with me so I can make you feel better." I lifted her chin and she smiled.

"Gage, I love you but if your brother is going to be there I'm not."

"He told me he was staying out."

"Are you sure?" I saw Maci pull up and I looked at Meadow.

"You called her?"

"You weren't here yet and I was ready to go."

"You coming Meadow."

"No I have her." Maci rolled her eyes and pulled off. I opened the door and Meadow got in. I didn't even bother to tell my mom I was leaving. The minute we got to my house she ran upstairs and hopped in the shower. I locked the door and turned everything off. I was on my way up when Khalid sent me a text telling me to get to the warehouse. I sent Meadow a text and told her I would be back and she better be ready for me.

"What up bro?" I asked Khalid when I walked in. Him and Bruno were eating pizza when I got there. They started telling me how one of the spots were hit and how another one was missing money. We were all shocked being no one ever stole from us. The three of us were running shit here in Connecticut, Boston, Ohio and a few other places. We didn't beef with too many motherfuckers that's why we never worried about anyone stealing from us. To hear the shit is happening is mind-boggling. We made plans to go over the tapes in every spot and find out who was working.

"How's it going with your brother over there?" Bruno asked and took a sip of soda.

"Good I guess. I never really see him."

"Do you think it's a good idea to have him around your girl?

"They never see each other either."

"Keep it that way. Does she know what he was in jail for?"

"Nah, I haven't told her."

"What the fuck is wrong with you?" Khalid jumped up mad. I know he looked at her like his sister. He has for a while now.

"Man, he's not going to fuck with her. Plus, I don't want her judging him for what he went down for."

"Man, you're bugging. Don't leave her at the house with him alone."

"Now you know I'm not stupid."

"Where is she now then?"

135

"At my house but Jesse is staying with my mom." I saw Khalid give me a crazy look.

"I see you and Meadow seem to be back on track." Bruno said trying to change the subject.

"Yea, I finally got her stubborn ass to tell me she loved me."

"Oh shit. That's what I'm talking about." Bruno gave me a high five. We kicked it a little longer and I headed home. I thought my ears were deceiving me when I heard moaning. But then I remember telling Meadow to be ready when I got there. She was probably playing with herself. I dropped my keys and ran up the steps. It was pitch dark in my room. I loved it that way; that's why I had black curtains and shades. I flicked the light on and almost lost my fucking mind.

"Somebody better tell me right fucking now what is going on?" I cocked my gun and placed it on my brothers' head.

"Oh my God." Meadow screamed out and kicked my brother in the face. She jumped off the bed and ran in the bathroom, slamming the door. My brother stood up and wiped his face off and turned around. I looked at him and his dick was out his pants too.

"Man, look. I came home to get some clothes and your girl was standing at the steps naked." I had to take a double take. My girl would never stand outside my room naked. But then again she did cook in just my t-shirt.

"I tried to walk into my room and she snatched me up by the shirt and told me she wanted me to eat her pussy and see if we were both good. I kept saying no but she stuck her fingers inside her pussy and put them in my mouth. Look man, I know you were feeling her but home girl is a hoe. I think you need to leave her alone."

"A hoe. Nah, Meadow isn't like that."

"Gage did you or did you not just catch me in between her legs. Did you hear her fighting me or telling me to get up? She only kicked me because you caught us. This isn't the first time either."

"What the fuck you mean this isn't the first time?"

"The day she made you breakfast she didn't have anything on underneath and had me eat her pussy in the

137

kitchen." This nigga was blowing my high with the stuff he was saying.

"Why didn't you tell me?"

"She begged me not to. Gage, we are brothers and you know I would never fuck your girl but she sure as hell doesn't feel the same." I was stuck like a motherfucker right now. I had my gun to my brothers' head and my girl in the bathroom screaming that he was lying, but was he? I mean she wasn't fighting or telling him to get off. I let my hand down and told him to go back to my mothers. When I heard the door shut I kicked the bathroom door off the hinges and Meadow was on the floor crying and shaking.

"Meadow, you have to go."

"What? Gage, tell me you don't believe him." I put my head down.

"Everything he said makes sense Meadow. You did cook in just my shirt and nothing under it."

"You told me he wasn't here."

"You weren't fighting him or telling him to get off either."

"Gage, listen to me. I came out the shower and got straight in the bed. I was still upset at what happened at your moms and just wanted to go to sleep. I shut the television off and you know how dark your room gets. Baby, you told me to wait for you so when I felt him under the covers I assumed it was you. Gage, he had just come in a few minutes before you walked in."

"You mean to tell me you don't know the difference."

"Gage, he had just bit down hard on my clit and I was trying to get away and ask what you were doing because you've never done that. He grabbed both of my legs and wouldn't allow me to move. I realized it wasn't you when I felt a beard on my calf but by then you had turned the light on."

"I don't know what to think Meadow."

"I get it. That's your brother and he said you would believe him before me." She stood up to walk away.

"What are you talking about?"

"Gage, he almost raped me at your mom's house and your mom was in on it." My head snapped back.

"Bitch, get out." I grabbed her by her hair and dragged

139

her back in the room.

"Gage, stop." She was trying to pry my hands from her hair.

"Put your clothes on. Matter of fact just go."

"Gage, please listen to me. Something is wrong with your brother and." I didn't hear anything else and smacked her across the face. She fell forward and hit the dresser.

"I better not ever see you again Meadow. I catch you in bed with my brother and now you're saying my mom helped him almost rape you. Get the fuck out." I picked her up by her head again and noticed blood coming down her leg. I figured her period must've come on.

"Oh my God Gage, I'm bleeding."

"I don't give a fuck."

"Gage, I'm pregnant." I let go of her hair, froze and gave her a mean stare.

"Whose baby is it?" She screamed out in pain and more blood started coming down. Her body was in a fetal position and she was turning blue. I thought about calling the ambulance but it would take them too long to get there. I wrapped the sheet around her and drove her to the hospital. I left her sisters number and walked out.

"Ma where are you?" I yelled out when I got in my mom's house.

"Why are you yelling boy?" She came out her bedroom and Jesse came out the bathroom.

"What happened over here when I left Meadow?"

"You mean when that skank called Jesse in the bathroom and then I heard some moaning going on?"

"Yea that."

"Honey, you need to let that go. Any woman that will sleep with brothers on purpose is a hoe." I was going to respond when my phone rang.

"What up Khalid?"

"Meet me at the hospital. Something happened to Meadow." I told him I would be there in a few. I left my moms and when I got to the hospital everyone was there. Her parents, my boys and Meadow's sisters. I walked over to greet them when Melina stood up.

"What the fuck are you here for?" She said with pure

venom in her voice.

"I dropped her off."

"What?" Khalid and Bruno both said at the same time. I pulled them to the side and explained what happened and Khalid and I almost fought had Bruno not pulled a gun on both of us and told us to calm down.

"You know dam well she didn't do that." Bruno tried to say but I wasn't trying to hear it.

"Jesse said that." I tried to get out.

"Fuck that rapist." I looked up at Khalid when he said that.

"Hold the fuck up. Your brother is a rapist and you allowed him around my sister." Maci said and started punching me. Their dad came over and grabbed her.

"My sister just lost her baby, your baby because you allowed him to come in and basically rape her. I think you should leave Gage and don't worry about speaking to her. Trust me when I say she doesn't want to have anything to do with you ever again." Melina said.

"What do you want me to do? That's my brother and."

"It doesn't even matter at this point Gage. You proved where your loyalty was and that's fine. I'm sure you don't have a problem walking away now that she lost the baby. I mean there's really no need for you to stick around." Maci shouted at me.

I felt like shit because I know that was my baby? She did tell me she wanted to talk to me about something? I wonder if that was it. What if my brother was lying? I thought about staying anyway but I didn't want to hear them talking shit. I got up and walked out the door. Maci was right it was no need for me to be there.

Khalid

I had just finished making love to Maci when both of our phones rang. That was unusual until we saw hers was from Melina and mine was form Bruno. We both assumed she was in labor and took a quick shower before we called them back. Imagine our surprise when we realized it wasn't her in labor but Meadow was there. No one knew what happened because the hospital refused to release any information on the phone. I called up Gage assuming he didn't know; come to find out he was the one who dropped her off. Notice how I said dropped her off and then left her. Who the fuck does that to the woman they love? He and I almost came to blows when he told me what the hell happened. I may not know her that well but I damn sure know her well enough to know his brother was lying his ass off. I told him not to allow her anywhere around that fucking rapist.

As you can tell I can't stand that punk ass nigga. Jesse was arrested ten years ago because he broke into someone's house attempting to rob them for who knows what reason. Jesse was not a boss like us but he was well paid and didn't want for shit. I guess they say you're the product of your own environment. That was his hustle before we made it big and I wasn't knocking it. Anyway, he broke in the house and the woman must've been in the shower. This idiot gets undressed and gets in there with her like she invited her. She goes to scream and the motherfucker grabs her by the throat and still has sex with her. This is what the woman stated in court. She told the judge it went on for a month until she finally got the courage up to set his stupid ass up and put cameras up in her house. The judge let the video play and he raped her in every hole and did things to her that should've been illegal.

Like the big brother that he is Gage hired him the best lawyer and he only got ten years for burglary. They didn't even charge him with the rape. The judge said he didn't know he was being taped and it was against the law. What kind of shit is that? I told Gage when he first told me Jesse was coming home to keep him away and tell her. But no, he didn't want her to judge him. He was rehabilitated and should have to be discriminated against. Now look at this shit. I don't care what he says that punk caused this. I was on my way to find out what really happened.

Meadow had been out the hospital for a week now since it happened and she was staying with Maci and I. It wasn't that she didn't want to be with her parents but Melina was about to have the baby and she didn't want to be a burden. No one knew she was with us and that's the way we wanted it. She changed her phone number and deleted any social media sites she had. Maci and I left her alone but you could hear her crying at night over what happened. I wanted to beat the hell out of Gage and his brother but that was my boy before she and I became cool.

"Hey you two." Maci leaned back on me as I sat and Meadow stayed on the loveseat.

"Meadow. I know it's been a rough week but can you tell us what happened." Maci and I were floored by what she said. The nigga's mom was on some other shit. I can't say I understand what Gage is going through but I get it. His girl telling him about his brother and mom and then they're telling him something totally different. I told her she was safe with us and she can believe he won't find her there but she said she was ready to go home. I think she was missing Gage. I know for sure he was missing the hell out of her. He and I only spoke when it dealt with business but I could tell how miserable he was. Bruno told me he asked about her a few times but he didn't have an answer. He had no idea where she was either.

Another week went by and I dropped Maci off to help Meadow get herself situated back at her house. I checked all the rooms and closets but Meadow assured me that he didn't know where she stayed but with a nigga like him one can never be too sure. I pulled Maci close to me and told her I was tearing that ass up later. She and I have been fucking like crazy. I wouldn't be surprised if she's next with a baby bump. I didn't plan it but I'm not strapping up either.

"I love you Maci and call me if there's a problem."

"I love you too. Are we ordering take out for dinner?"

"I'm probably going to be out late so take Meadow out." I handed her money and she left it on the passenger seat.

"Maci, take this money."

"No Khalid. Go to work and don't make me come looking for you." I smiled and pulled off. I went to the warehouse first and one of the guys had me looking at the videos of the trap houses. You could see someone come in with a gun and rob one of them but then the same person came in and knew exactly where to look in the other one. You couldn't see their face because it was covered in a ski mask and he had a hoodie on. It was something about the way he moved that was familiar. I'm sure I'll figure it out. When someone is robbing you most of the time its someone you already know.

It was a little after nine when I got to the club. I was going over some of Meadows paperwork for her accounting firm. We had to push the grand opening back due to what happened to her. She had another month before it would happen. She wanted all the same people to attend and to make that happen it would be that long. People had to rearrange their schedules but it was what she wanted. My door slammed and I looked up and she stood their stripping. My dick got hard right away.

"What are you doing here?" I put my tongue in her mouth and then sucked on her breast one by one.

"I needed to see you."

"I can tell." I let my hand go in her undercarriage and the heat was brewing down there for sure."

"Khalid."

"Yea." I unbuttoned my pants to release the beast and couldn't get it out quick enough.

"I think I'm pregnant." It was like everything in the room stopped.

"Are you sure or is it just a thought?" I leaned back in my chair staring at her.

"I'm almost positive I am. I have all the symptoms and I haven't gotten my period since we started sleeping together." She kissed on my neck and I moved her back.

"What do you want to do?"

"I'm keeping it." She said and guided herself down on my pole.

"Shittttt. You feel so good."

"How good." I lifted her up and down on it.

"Real good. Make me cum." She went faster and started yelling out my name. She knows I loved hearing her.

"I love you Khalid." I stopped her and looked in her eyes.

"Marry me Maci." She nodded her head yes and started crying. I told her to stay just like she was and reached in my drawer and pulled out the six carat emerald diamond ring I got her. I had it for some time now but was waiting for the right moment. I would say her announcing that she's pregnant is a good time.

"Oh my God Khalid. When did you get this?"

"It doesn't matter. You said yes and that's all that counts." I slid in on her finger and let her ride me into a damn coma. I taught her so well she started doing her own tricks. I took her in my bathroom and washed both of us up and proposed to her the right way. Shit, my dick was still in her when I asked.

"Maci, I fell in love with you the first time I saw you. I made it my business to stay around you and when you left me my heart was broke. Just know that you are my world and no one will ever come before you or my kids. I love you will you marry me?"

"Yes again baby." We kissed until we heard someone clearing their throats. I turned around and it was Meadows crazy ass. She noticed it before Maci got to say it and started screaming and jumping up and down with her. I loved seeing my girl happy and I wasn't about to allow anyone to mess it up.

"How long are you staying Maci?"

"I don't know. Why you got some other chick coming?"

"Nah, but my fiancé may show up." I grinned and she smiled and kissed me. The two of them walked downstairs and ended up on the dance floor. I took glances every now and then to make sure no one was bothering them. I saw one person I didn't want to and tried to make it down there but I was too late.

"He put a ring on it boo so beat your feet." I heard Maci saying when I walked up.

"What does that mean? I just sucked his dick last week here." *Fuck, this bitch be doing too much.*

"And you're proud of that? What does that say about you? You sucked his dick and he still didn't wife you." I heard people in the crowd cheering Maci on. I knew she was pissed but she wasn't about to allow Maribel to get the best of her either.

"Go head and marry him. I bet I still has me bent over on that burgundy desk he got upstairs." Maci didn't bat and eye but I was pissed.

"You just said you sucked his dick."

"Yup but a few weeks ago I was getting my ass busted in that office. Damn, he does have that dope dick right?"

"The same desk I just fucked him all over. Yea, see this man right here isn't about to allow some hoe that cheated on him to be his wife. But I'll do a great job just so you know." Maci stood in front of me.

"Do you boo? I'll be the best side chick in the world because we'll be sharing baby daddies for real this time."

"Great, make sure you call me for play time." I could see the anger in Maribel's face. She was not getting under Maci's skin and it was killing her. I nodded my head towards security and they threw her stupid ass out. The music was still popping and I'm sure only a few people heard what happened but the fact that Meadow was there and gave me the look of disgust hurt me. I would never disrespect Maci and everyone knew that but this shit that Maribel said was the ultimate.

"I'm moving back home." She said in my ear and kissed me on the dance floor as if nothing happened.

"No you're not."

"You broke your promise Khalid. You told me you would never allow anyone to approach me. I hate you so much right now I want to slap you but I'm going to save face and act like it's all good like I've been doing. Stay the fuck away from me OK." She kissed my lips and went towards Meadow who was at the bar.

****

I ran upstairs to lock my office up and take Maci home but she must've bounced before I came back. I played it cool and gave the bartender a handshake and stepped outside. That stupid bitch was outside smoking a cigarette with a grin on her face. I walked over to her slowly and chuckled.

"Another one bites the dust." She blew smoke in my face.

"They crack so easy Khalid. You need to find a woman who is not so weak. She should've known I was lying knowing you're not a cheating nigga. Even I know that but I guess she didn't trust you after all."

"What makes you think she left me?"

"Ugh, the way she stormed out of here. I see she waited a bit before she did though to make it seem like she wasn't mad." I didn't even answer her stupid ass.

"Why don't you want me to be happy Maribel? Just make me understand." I asked leaning up against the wall. Maribel was a good girlfriend but she cheated and there would never be an us.

"Because if you're going to be happy without me make it with a bitch who can fuck with me. You know I'm childish. It's what I do. Khalid you are going to make a great husband, father, provider and all that. But if every woman you pick can't trust you off the shit I say then there's no need to be with her."

I hate to admit it but Maribel was right. I told Maci a hundred times Maribel was childish and would do anything to mess with her. The way Maci just believed her and didn't even question if I lied or not had me thinking if I made the right choice proposing. Yes, I loved her with all my heart but did she love me. How could she when she was tested and failed miserably? Not saying I knew Maribel would say that crazy shit but she did leave. Fuck it; I'm tired of fighting to stay with her. She's going to believe what she wants if she wants me then she's going to have to show me it's worth it.

"Bye Maribel."

"Bye boo. I'll be around to run away the next one. Love ya." She laughed and went to her car. That chick was crazy but she made sense and I couldn't be mad at her.

Maci

I stormed out the club not because I believed her stupid ass but because Khalid still has yet to put an end to the shit. I know for a fact she was lying that's why when Maribel continued talking I went along with her. She loved trying to get under my skin. I caught on to her childish ways a while ago. But he did break his promise to me and that was not allowing anyone to approach me with bs. I loved the hell out of Khalid but until he put an end to the madness I was taking a break.

"You keeping the ring on?" Meadow asked me when we got back to the house.

"Ugh yea. We're still getting married."

"You know he's going to come get you."

"No I don't think so."

"Why not?" She said and closed the door.

"Because he's trying to figure out what to say and how to get that chick to leave me alone."

"Do you believe her?"

"Not one bit. My baby didn't even go to the club last week and when he did leave guess who was his passenger? That's right his wife."

"You his wife already?"

"I've been his wife. Girl you ain't know. You better ask somebody."

"What about her saying he had her bent over on his burgundy desk?"

"The bitch is so stupid. If she was really up there she would know he got rid of that one months ago and he has a black one now." Women are so dumb. If you're going to lie at least make it believable. He told me that desk was bad luck because Maribel picked it out and he didn't want anything reminding him of her.

Meadow and I ordered some take out and watched

London has fallen which was a great movie. I took a nice hot bath and went to check on Meadow. I could hear her sniffling and got in bed with her.

"I miss him Maci."

"I know sis and he misses you too." She rolled over and asked me how I knew. I told her Khalid told me when he sees him he looks miserable and has been asking about her. I know he was conflicted with who to believe. Once we heard the entire story from my sister who could blame him? It doesn't excuse him putting his hands on her. He didn't make her lose the baby like we assumed either. She was almost three months and the stress that she was under made her miscarry. Evidently, she was already in the process of losing it that night. We couldn't blame him for that because it was his brother that had her like that.

"You think I should call him?"

"Honestly no. I don't want you to think I'm being mean. But sis he did put his hands on you and if you decide to take him back that's your choice. But at least make him work for you. Don't be that woman begging him to take you back when

157

you did nothing wrong. Let him beg for your forgiveness and if you choose to allow him back in your life then you know I'll be right here to support you. Plus, I don't think he hit you on purpose. I think hearing his mom and brother basically worked together to do that to you made him snap."

"I'm sure it did. Can you believe his mom cosigned it? I wonder if she loves Gage. She can't if she allowed her other son to do that to his girl right?"

"I don't know sis. It's crazy but some parents do crazy things for their kids. You know daddy was ready to kill Gage until mom had to throw it on him to keep him calm."

"Yuk Maci."

"What Melina told me she had to ask Bruno if she could stay the night because she couldn't take hearing dad moaning?"

"Dad."

"Yup your father."

"Ok. Get it mom." We shared a laugh and both fell asleep. A week went by and still no word from Khalid. I wasn't thinking anything bad but a bitch, no his fiancé was definitely showing up at the crib unannounced. I waited until after two in the morning, hopped my ass in the car and drove over there. All the lights were out but there was another car in the driveway. I put my key in the door and closed it quietly. I didn't think he would sleep with anyone else but this other car made me think different. I locked up and went in his room. His ass was knocked out with the television on.

I moved the covers back slightly and he was wearing just boxers and his print was showing. I went and locked the bedroom door. Ever since my sister told me that peeping tom did that I wasn't taking any chances. I removed my shoes and pulled his dick through the hole and sucked him so good he woke up out his sleep.

"I missed you Maci." He didn't even open his eyes. My baby knew who was giving him the business and that's all that mattered to me.

"I don't want to cum in your mouth. I want to feel inside. Come sit on your dick." I did as he asked and both of us let go at the same time.

"Baby can you wash us up?"

"What's wrong? Why are you slurring?" I came out the bathroom with the rag waiting on him to answer. He told me him and Gage had a talk and we're taking shots. I figured that's who the other car belonged too but it must've been new because I've never saw that one. He just got in the bed when I got there and was too tired to get back up. I was happy they made up but with Gage's brother still out there I'm not sure how long that's going to last.

"Maci you leaving."

"Yes."

"Why?"

"You need to put a muzzle on that chick."

"Come here baby." He pulled me close to him.

"You know I didn't sleep with her."

"Yes I do. I know she was saying anything to get under my skin. This is my dick and I will know if you step out. But the fact remains that you broke your promise."

"I know and I'm going to handle her. I'm sure you're tired of her approaching you. I thought she would stop but I was wrong." He lifted my shirt and kissed my belly.

160

"You still have your ring on."

"Of course. I was the wife before I got this."

"That you were baby. Now get in the bed with me. I haven't been sleeping good since you've been gone."

"Oh no."

"No. I want to make love to you Maci but my body is so tired that's why I had you ride me. I promise to make it up to you."

"It's ok baby. I still love you." I kissed his lips and snuggled up under him.

I woke up the next day and Khalid was gone. I glanced at my phone and it was after twelve. This baby had me sleeping my life away. I dialed Khalid's phone and he walked in the room with some food for me. It was grits, bacon, toast, pancakes and sausages. It was so much I offered him some.

"Baby I have a doctor's appointment at three."

"Ok well start getting ready. You know how long it takes you."

We got to the doctors at two thirty and signed in. I had to fill out a ton of forms first. At least the wait wasn't longer than ten minutes. The nurse took us in the back and did my vitals and had me undress from the waist down. Khalid's nasty ass wanted to have sex with my legs in the stirrups. I told him he was crazy but if that's what he wanted then he should have one sent to the house.

The doctor walked in and introduced herself. After talking for a few minutes she turned the machine on, inserted the device and showed us our baby. Khalid had the biggest grin on his face. I was six weeks pregnant which is exactly how long I've been sleeping with him. I got pregnant the night he broke my virginity. Ain't that some shit. The doctor gave me the prescription for vitamins and told me to have the nurse schedule me an appointment for one month out.

"Well, well, well. What are you two doing here?" Maribel said walking towards the building while we went to our car.

"Checking on our little one and you bitch."

"Bitch."

"Yes bitch. Make this your last time addressing me." I went to walk away and Khalid pulled me back.

"Maribel, you've gotten away with a lot of shit and I haven't said anything. Like she said make this your last time addressing her. You may not take her threats serious but I know you will take mine. If I hear you as so much look at my fiancé the wrong way its lights out."

"Khalid you would kill me?"

"Over her I would. Goodbye Maribel." He took my hand and led me back to his ride. I didn't say two words as I could see he was in his thoughts. He opened the door and I locked it. I went straight in the bathroom to shower. I hated when the GYN put the gel on their fingers and in your vagina.

"Come here Maci." I dried off and went in the room like I was in trouble.

"Yea."

"Bring my pussy to me so I can eat. It's been a week since I've tasted you." I dropped my towel and allowed him to have his way with me.

Meadow

Maci told me she was going to creep up on Khalid and she'd be back. That was over a week ago and I ain't seen the heffa since. She has face timed me every day and night to check on me and Khalid makes her hang up. He claims to need all her attention until the baby gets here. Melina was eight and a half months now and she was huge. Bruno was still trying to get her back and she was making him work for it like crazy.

He had to bring her food whenever she wanted, cater to her every move and she was not giving him any sex unless he got tested. He did that immediately and she still didn't give him any. I told her she better stop playing with him before he go out and find someone else. She claimed she didn't care but we knew they were still in love with each other.

It's been about a month since that mess happened and I was still missing the hell out of Gage. Today was my grand opening and I was so excited. Khalid and Maci were picking me up in an hour and I had to get in the shower. I put my brand new white pantsuit on with a corset top that boosted the heck out of my boobs. I grabbed my white red bottoms. My hair is was in curls flowing down my back. My makeup was light and last but not least I sprayed a vanilla scent on me. That was my favorite of all time.

I heard the horn blow and grabbed everything I needed. I spoke to those two fools who were dressed alike in Versace. There were a ton of cars lined up. Thank goodness my dad paid for cops to be out there directing traffic. I walked in and the music was playing, wine was being passed around, the hord'oeuvres were out and the people were mingling. Bruno came up and introduced me to some of his so called people who needed help going over there books. As long as they paid me well I could care less how they made it. I handed them a card and kept it moving. I noticed one of them eye fucking the hell out of me. I was good on that. A few hours and many potential clients later I was beat.

"You ready sis?" Maci said when she came to my office.

"Yea let me lock up." She walked out. I heard the door open back to my office.

"Can I help you?" I was picking my phone up off the floor so I had no idea who it was. The person didn't say anything. I was a tad bit nervous to turn around. I was shocked and nervous at the same time.

"Do you have a minute?" He didn't wait for me to answer. He stepped in closer and cupped my face and his tongue became intertwined with mine. His kiss was so passionate it literally took my breath away. My arms found their way around his neck.

"Umm are we taking you home or is he?" I heard Maci say in the background. Neither of us stopped.

"Fine. Gage make sure she goes home. Call me Meadow." She slammed the door. He lifted me in his arms and sat me on the desk. I snatched my jacket off and he planted kisses on my neck. We were like animals in heat the way we went at it. I didn't even care how tired I was at this point. I just needed to feel him. The moment he entered me it was as if everything stopped. We stared at one another as he gave me stroke for stroke. My legs were on his shoulders and I couldn't help but scream out.

"Damn Meadow. I'm getting ready to cum already." I didn't say anything. I was happy because it meant he hadn't been sleeping with anyone if he came that quick. Well I hope not anyway. After he came I jerked him back to life and rode him until my body couldn't take anymore.

"Turn over." I did what he said and threw my ass back. After another half hour or so we both came and laid there on the floor in silence. I don't think either of us knew exactly what to say. My phone started ringing from an unknown number.

"Hello. Hello." I spoke twice in the phone and no one said anything. This had been going on for the last two weeks.

"Who was that?"

"I don't know. The number is private."

"Is that the first time they called you?"

"No. It's been for the past two weeks." It rang again and

he answered it. The person still didn't say anything and it pissed him off more.

"Get dressed." He demanded and I jumped up and did it. Maybe the person did say something. After we got dressed he waited for me to lock everything up and told me to get in the car. He stood outside on the phone but I could hear him saying something wasn't right. He was off by the time he sat down. At my house he didn't allow me to step out the car until he checked the entire house; inside and out.

"Meadow. Tell me if that number calls you again."

"Ok." He got in his car and left. I know this nigga didn't just hit it and run. Oh well it was definitely worth it. I locked up everything and went to take a bath.

My phone was ringing off the hook the next day. I glanced up to see what time it was and it was only seven in the morning. I snatched the phone and saw that it was from a private number again. I shut the shit off. I tried to go back to sleep but sleep did not come back for me. I did my daily routine and headed to my mom's house.

"Bitch, where you been?" Maci asked parking behind

168

me. I didn't even get a chance to go in my parents' house yet.

"Home. Why?"

"I've been calling you all morning to tell you Melina went into labor." I patted my pants and checked my purse and realized I left it at home. I hopped in the car with her and we got to the hospital in no time. The labor and delivery floor was on the fourth floor and it seemed like it took us forever to get there. We were both excited to be an auntie. The elevator door opened and my parents and I'm guessing his parents and Khalid were all outside.

"It's about time. Where have you been?" I didn't realize anyone else called. I shut the phone off without paying attention. My mom, his mom, Maci and me went in the back and Bruno looked like he was ready to pass out. He thanked us for coming in and walked back out. Melina told us he was nervous and scared. He said too many people died during birth and there was no way he would watch her die in front of him. He was being extra dramatic but it is what it is.

"Let's see how many centimeters you are Ms. Woods." The doctor came in smiling. She told my sister she was at nine and it was time to get prepared for the delivery. We watched the bottom half of the bed go down and Melina move closer to the edge. My mom and his mom were on each side of her. Maci was recording her and I stood there watching in awe. To see another human come out was crazy. Eight hours later Melina pushed out Morgan Karissa Jackson. She weighed nine pounds two ounces and still appeared to be super tiny.

"She is tiny as hell." Khalid said as he peeked over Maci's shoulder while she held her. He stepped out to answer his phone then gestured for me to come out there. He passed me the phone and told me to stop making his brother call everywhere for her. I had no idea what he was talking about.

"Hello."

"Meadow where's your phone?" *Damn I didn't get a hello or anything.*

"I left it at home by accident. That private number called again and woke me up out of my sleep. I shut it off and left without it."

"I've been looking for you all day."

"You could've just called your boy."

"I didn't think you were with him." I was about to say something when I turned around to see him standing there.

"Why would you call and you knew you were coming up here?" I pushed him in the chest and laughed.

"Because I can do that." He hugged me and planted a kiss on my lips. We walked in the room and all eyes were on us. Bruno's mom gave him a hug and my parents just nodded at him. My folks were pretty easy going but we were their life. I'm sure they're still not over what happened. Another hour went by and visiting hours were over. I didn't want to leave but Bruno told us to get out so he could bond with his daughter. He just ought to being she was his damn twin.

"I'll see you later Gage."

"Nah, you're coming with me." He had his hand in mine.

"Gage, I'm not going to that house." He turned around and pulled me close.

"Meadow, I would never ask you to return somewhere that makes you uncomfortable. I want to take you to dinner and then I have a surprise for you."

"You do." My smile grew wide as I followed him.

"Have fun sis and enjoy the surprise."

"You know what it is?"

"Ugh, yea. Khalid tried to keep it from me but I fucked the shit out of him and he told me." I smacked her on the arm. Now that she was no longer a virgin you would swear she was a porn star. We said our goodbyes to them and I got in the car with him to go to dinner. He pulled up to the cheesecake factory and I just about ran in. I hadn't been here in weeks and this was me and my sisters' favorite place to eat. I ordered a salad that he and I shared. If you've ever eaten there you know they give you a lot of food. Afterwards, I ordered the Pasta da Vinci for my entrée and he ordered Cajun Jambalaya Pasta.

"Meadow, let me start off by saying I apologize from the bottom of my heart for putting my hands on you." I dropped my fork when he said that. It wasn't anything I wanted to talk about but to have a boss nigga apologizing was huge for a small time girl like me.

I heard all about Khalid, Bruno and Gage. Those are three niggas no one ever wanted beef with. They had an army of soldiers ready to go to war for them with one phone call. I've also heard about how people go missing if you do them wrong; like steal or cheat from them. It was crazy seeing him vulnerable with me and I loved it.

"When I saw you two my mind was going crazy. I didn't know what to think or who to believe but when you mentioned my mom I snapped. When you said you were pregnant I knew it my heart the baby was mine but I was too far gone by then. I want to apologize for you having a miscarriage. I will never forgive myself for making you lose our first child."

"Gage, the baby died due to me being stressed out about what was going on with your brother and me getting ready for the grand opening." I could've let him believe it was his fault but I wasn't built like that.

"WHAT?" He yelled out making people look.

"Gage, calm down. It's ok. I got through it." I had my hand on his.

"It's not ok." I glanced around the restaurant and saw two dudes nod their head at him.

"Gage, are they with you?"

"No. They're for you."

"For me. Why?"

"Once you told me about the phone call I started having someone following you. Meadow I don't care if you hate me and never want to see me again after tonight. But one thing I won't do is allow anything else to happen to you. I know I messed up bad but you are still my everything and always will be."

"Gage, that's really nice of you to say and do."

"I don't know what I would do if anything happened to you. I know you may not believe me but I had a meltdown when you lost our baby. All I wanted to do was be there for you but your family was not having it. I didn't even know where you were for the first two weeks until I spoke to my boy who by the way was ready to fight me over you. Can you believe that? We been brothers forever but he was ready to have a brawl over you. I understand it though. I would do the same if it was Melina or Maci."

"Gage, do you think that I let your brother do those

174

things to me willingly?" I had to know; I wanted to hear what he had to say. He leaned back and put his hands on top of his head and let out a deep breath before he spoke. Whatever he was about to say was weighing heavy on him.

"I believed you Meadow. I always have. If you would've told me what happened at my mom's house I could've handled it better than walking in on it. Seeing it made me think it was true. Then he started saying things to make me look at you sideways but baby I knew. I just couldn't handle it and that's why I'm so fucked up over it." I felt the tears falling as he said it. All this time I thought he believed I would cheat on him. He took my hands in his.

"I'm about to tell you something and I pray you don't get mad." I wiped my face and waited for him to speak. His phone rang and he told me to hold on while he answered it.

"We have to go."

"But you said you had to tell me something."

"Baby, I'll tell you later." The two guys came to where we were and escorted me out the back of the restaurant, which was weird because I didn't even know they could do that. I sat

175

in the back of a black Yukon with tinted windows. I heard the guys on the phone then twenty minutes later we drove around the same block three or four times before we parked in front of some house. The passenger went in the house first and then came back out handing me the keys. I stepped out and went inside. I noticed they never left.

There were marble floors and cathedral ceilings throughout the downstairs. The kitchen was huge as was the living room. There was a room you walked down into I assumed was a family room. There was a huge television on the wall and a sectional that took up damn near the entire room. I looked through the doors and there was two full bathrooms downstairs and a basement that I was scared to look in. I strolled my nosy ass upstairs and it had to be at least seven bedrooms by the amount of doors I counted. Every room was empty except two. One had an office in it with top of the line office equipment. I mean there was a fax machine, a copy machine, an apple computer with an apple laptop and iPad next to it. There were two televisions in there, a closet and bathroom.

I closed the door and went into the last bedroom, which I assumed was the master bedroom. I covered my mouth when I looked in. The bed was at least a California king canopy if not bigger. The television had to be over seventy inches. I went in the bathroom and there was a shower and bath with two doors with two toilets in them.

The closet was filled with clothes, shoes and purses. I went to the balcony and there were glass windows overlooking a lake in the backyard. I saw a Jacuzzi and pool outside too. Whoever house this was had it laid out. Except for the empty rooms. I was on my way out when I noticed and envelope on the dresser with my name on it. I opened it and almost passed out. The deed to the house was in my name. Last but not least there were two other titles to a brand new Porsche truck and a new Mercedes CLS 550.

Meadow,

If you're reading this that means you just realized you had a house and new cars. I know this won't make up for how I treated you but I wanted you to know that it doesn't end here. I am going to do whatever I can to get you back in my life.

I love you

Gage

I dropped on the floor and started crying. I heard the door open and close and there were my parents, the guys from the truck, Maci, Khalid and Melina and Bruno were on face time with Maci. I wasn't sure if something happened to Gage and it took all of them to tell me.

"Is Gage ok?" I ran down the steps and almost busted my ass.

"I'm fine baby." He came out in an all-black tuxedo with a small black pillow in his hand. There was a huge diamond ring on top. I covered my mouth and looked around. Everyone was already staring at me.

"Meadow."

"Yes Gage Yes."

"Shut up Meadow. Let him get it out." Melina said making everyone laugh.

"Thank you Melina." He told her.

"Meadow, the first day I saw you all I thought about

178

was sleeping with you. Funny how it happened though." He snickered.

"Anyway, before you no woman in my twenty eight years made me fall in love with them. After being around you my feelings started changing and you made me want to be a better man. I fell in love with you and then you became my everything. I couldn't wait to get home to you every day. You are the only woman I want to wake up to for the rest of my life. Will you marry me?" I had so many tears falling down my face my vision was blurry. He slid the ring on my finger and lifted me up to kiss me. I heard everyone clapping and my parents gave me a hug.

"Congratulations sis. I have to go because your niece wants to eat." Melina said and blew me a kiss.

"Do you like your house?" My sister Maci asked me.

"I did a good job picking it right?"

"You picked this? I thought you said you had to sleep with Khalid to find out the surprise."

"I knew about the house but he had to tell me about the ring."

"This house though."

"Yup. Gage gave me a price range and this is what I got. Can you believe no one ever lived here? Some man had it built for his wife a year ago but she passed away unexpectedly and he didn't want to live in it. Fuck it. We're about to party up in here." She grabbed my hand and took me out in the back.

"Sis, I know you're still on your high but I want to say something to you."

"What's wrong?" I could see in her face it wasn't going to be good.

"Meadow, Gage is in love with you and while I don't agree with what he did his heart is beating just for you. He has something to tell you but when he does you have to hear him out. It's going to shock you at first and probably have you flipping because I did. Just know that he would never intentionally put you in harm's way." I nodded my head and sat there staring into the darkness. I was worried about what this news was. It had to be bad if he got her to sit me down first.

"Congratulations baby." My dad said and came to sit

180

next to me. He and I talked about everything and then my mom came out and did the same. I noticed everyone was inside drinking and all I wanted to do was lie down in my new bed. It had gold satin sheets with a thick ass gold comforter. I told Gage I was going upstairs and gave everyone a hug. I turned on the bath and stripped to get in. The jets were massaging my body and I ended up falling asleep in there. I felt someone lift me out and lay me on the bed still wrapped in my towel. I heard the shower cut on and I figured he was staying over. *Wait, does that mean he lives with me?* I laughed at myself.

"Do you mind if I stay the night?" He asked before he got in the bed.

"I want you to stay forever." He leaned in to kiss me.

"Sounds like a plan. I'm looking at you Meadow and all I want to do is make love to you." I unwrapped my towel and told him to go for it. He said what he wanted to tell me earlier had to be said before anything.

"Baby, I want you to know I would never do anything to put you in danger. I love you so much and I would murder anyone for fucking with you."

"I know Gage. What's wrong?"

"Promise me you won't leave me."

"Why would I leave you?"

"Just promise."

"Ok I promise." As he told me what his brother did and why he was in jail I found myself crying hysterical. I wanted to smack him and beat on him but that's not me. He wrapped his arms around me while I cried. After I stopped I asked him why his mom would allow him to do that to me. I could tell his mom was still a sensitive spot but she still allowed it.

"I don't know Meadow. I'm going to say she did because he may have lied and said you wanted him. I know this sounds crazy but I haven't been able to look at either one of them. I went by there the night it all went down and they called you all these names. It was as if they both hated you but that couldn't be when you just met. I will never allow them to bother you again baby. Please understand how hard it was for me at first but I need you to know that I would never ever put you in a room with him alone."

"I know Gage. He wasn't supposed to be there and I

know how you felt about me."

"But I need you to know that, that better be the only thing you kept from me. I can't take any more lies or deceit. I can't say you lied because I never asked you why he was in there but as your woman you had the responsibility to tell me something like that. You may not have left me in a room with him but you left the door open for him to feel comfortable doing it. And I mean that figuratively speaking."

"I'm sorry and it will never happen again. I do need you to tell me if you ever see him around you or if he calls you."

"He shouldn't. I have a new number and no one knows I live here right."

"No."

"Gage, I want a baby with you in the future."

"We can get started right now."

"Ugh, no. Your ass is in time out for a week. Then and maybe then I'll think about giving you some." I kissed his lips and got in the bed naked.

"So you're just going to lay there naked. That's fucked

up."

"You're good baby." I put pillows in between us and he moved them and grabbed my body to him. He climbed on top of me and started kissing on my chest and made his way down to my love box. I lost count of how many times I came.

"Gage, what did I say? Shit baby." I moaned out when I felt the head of his penis at my entrance. A few seconds later he pushed himself in.

"Yup. That time out shit can start tomorrow. I'm making love to you tonight." And that's exactly what he did.

Melina

I gave birth to my daughter four weeks ago and I have enjoyed every single second of being a mother. The only thing I hated was Morgan was a spitting image of Bruno. I guess it's true when the say the person you couldn't stand the most in your pregnancy will have your child looking just like them. The only thing that she had of mine was my blue eyes. Her father hated that because he said all those hardheaded boys are going to be lusting after her. He was so overprotective of her that no one was allowed to take her anywhere unless it was in my parents' house or if I took her out. His mom had to yell at him when we went by there because he didn't want her taking Morgan out the car seat.

I was taking her to the doctors today to get her four-week checkup and I think she's getting some shots. I didn't want her dad to come because like I said he's so overprotective that I'm sure he's going to flip. I put on a cute tutu with a onesie shirt that said I love my daddy. I put a headband on her head and some small Jordan's Gage brought her. This girl is beyond spoiled.

I parked in front of the doctors' office and spotted Bruno talking on the phone. He came to where I parked and took Morgan out the seat and carried her in; leaving me with the stroller. We sat there for about ten minutes before the nurse called us.

"Morgan Jackson."

"Here we are." The nurse stepped aside so we could go in. She had us undress Morgan and put her on the scale. We answered a few questions and waited on the doctor. Once the doctor came in I didn't have to open my mouth because her dad did.

"Wow. I haven't seen too many dads be able to answer every question."

"Please don't get him started doc." I said sucking my

teeth.

"Don't get mad Melina." He said and smirked.

"Boy please. You only know because you spoil her and if Morgan makes a small noise or cries you come running over to the house like someone killing her."

"So. She doesn't need to cry."

"I see this is your first baby." The doctor said getting Morgan's arm ready for the shot. Bruno must not have been paying her any mind but he damn sure flipped when Morgan screamed out.

"Yo what the fuck? Why would you stab her in the arm like that? Let me get the fuck out of here before I kill your dumb ass."

"Bruno stop it. You're scaring the doctor and Morgan does not need to hear you talking like that." Thank goodness she only had one shot because he was not going to allow another one. I got Morgan dressed and apologized to the doctor on the way out. I had to tell her he was bi polar just so she wouldn't call the cops. We ended up going by Meadows new house and I had them on the floor cracking up when I told them how Bruno was acting.

"Really Bruno." Meadow said taking Morgan from him.

"Fuck that. No one puts their hands on my baby." He popped up and told Gage to go outside with him; he needed a smoke to calm down. Meadow and I kept laughing at his crazy ass. I noticed my sisters' phone going off while she was in the kitchen so I answered it.

"Hello."

"You can run but you can't hide."

"Who is this?"

"Don't worry Meadow. Your time is coming."

"This isn't Meadow. Who the fuck is this?" The person started laughing and hung up. I ran outside and told the guys. Gage took the phone from me to get the number but it was private. He was livid and before I knew it he was coming down the steps with a scowl on his face.

"Gage what's wrong? Why are you dressed like that?" I hadn't told Meadow anything and he asked me not too. He didn't want her stressing herself out.

"I have some things to handle baby that's all. I want you

to go with Melina to your parents' house."

"But I don't want to. I have work to do." He pulled her close to him.

"Can you please do this for me? I promise I'll make it up to you." Once he whispered something in her ear she smiled and nodded her head. I was happy to see them together even though he was on my shit list for putting his hands on her. He genuinely was in love with my sister and no one could deny that.

"You ok Meadow." I noticed her staring out the window.

"I think Gage's brother is the one playing on my phone."

I shut the car off when we pulled in at the house. I asked her why she felt that way and she told me Jesse told her that he was jealous of her sleeping with his brother and how he couldn't wait for her to sit on his face. I asked her if she mentioned it to her man and when she told me no I could've smacked the hell out of her. I have heard so many stories of women holding things in because they thought they could handle it or didn't want their man to go after the person. Unfortunately, it doesn't always turn out good for the chick that didn't say anything.

She stayed at the house until Gage came and got her. I called Bruno and told him what she said and he was mad as hell. He said Gage thinks it's him too but he can't find him. They went by his moms' house and she claims to have not seen him in a few weeks.

"Come outside Melina." I peeked out the window and Bruno was standing there. I put my slippers and robe on. I wasn't worried about Morgan because my mom said she was keeping her in the room with them.

"Get in the car."

"Bruno I'm not dressed."

"Now Melina." I pouted but got in. He parked the truck in front of his house and told me to get out. I followed him inside and noticed he had brand-new everything. I was just there two weeks ago and it didn't look like this. I heard him lock the doors behind me and go upstairs. Who told this nigga I was staying here? I heard the water running and assumed he was in the shower. I went in the room and he had so much steam coming out the bathroom from the hot water I went to shut the door. I saw his body through the glass door and stood there. It's not like I never saw it before but it had been so long since I've been with a man a bitch was horny. I took my slippers, robe and pajamas off and slid the door open. He didn't even turn around and continued washing up.

"It's about time." He said and looked at me. I stood on my tippy toes to kiss him and seconds later he was pulling my second orgasm out with his mouth. The first one came almost the second he touched her. He stuck his finger inside and my body shook until I finished. I wanted to give him head but I wasn't ready. He lifted me up and had my pussy spread open as I glided down on him.

"Oh shit Bruno. It's been so long it hurts."

"It's ok baby. I'll go slowly." I bit down on his neck as he helped me get used to him again.

"Melina, this pussy has to be the best I ever had. Fuck, all I want to do is live in it."

"This is the best dick I ever had too baby. Fuck me like

it's your last time." He turned the shower off and stepped out with me still on his dick. He had me screaming and running from him.

"Melina cum on your dick again. I love seeing that shit." The minute he said it I released and so did he. I guess he couldn't hold out any longer.

"That pussy is still mine Melina. If you ever give it away I'm killing you."

"Damn Bruno."

"I mean that. I can't fathom the thought of someone getting a taste of you."

"Bruno you do know we're not together anymore right."

"Melina, you don't really have a choice."

"What is that supposed to mean?" I sat up and stared at him. He lit his blunt and blew smoke.

"You know exactly what it means."

"Bruno I didn't bother you when you was with that chick."

"Melina, go ahead and be with someone else and see what happens. Each one will die a tragic death."

"Bruno."

"Melina, do you like the way I make love to you? Or how I make that pussy talk and cry?"

"You know I do. No one has ever made my body feel like that."

"Then there's no need to go looking anywhere else now is it?" I rolled my eyes and turned over.

"Get your spoiled ass over here. Melina, you are still going to be my wife. You may as well get used to it." He put the blunt out and showed me again why there was no need to look anywhere else. I knew it and so did he.

Bruno

I know you guys haven't heard much from me but that's because I'm not a big talker. My girl Melina told you just about everything there is to know. She was my number one fan and that's why she was the only one that would carry my last name besides my daughter. Many women have tried to get me where she has but it was something about her that drew me in and that was before we had sex. I used to see her when I picked Khalid up and for some reason I was nervous as hell to talk to her. Melina was beautiful in my eyes and me being the rough neck nigga I am I figured she wouldn't give me the time of day. Fortunately I had her wrong and she was waiting for me to approach her.

Melina had everything going for her. She was in school, beautiful, banging ass body but her intellect is what caught me.

194

Yes she was in school but a lot of dumb people are in school. I appreciated how she could carry on a conversation and keep me interested. She knew the kind of work I did and never once nagged me if I didn't come home or called her. I think she was so caught up in school she probably didn't have time. But when we were together it was never about anyone or anything else but her. She always had my undivided attention.

I didn't tell my boys Khalid and Gage about her right away because she asked me not too. Meadow was not the woman that dealt with street dudes and Melina swore she would rat her out. I thought it was dumb but I respected it. When I saw those dudes at the table trying to talk to her at my boys party all I saw as red. Melina had the type of pussy to make me do that. I know people say pussy is pussy and they're right. But when you have a woman that can fuck the shit out of you and put you to sleep; you need to lock her down. I still remember the first time I dug in her. It was so good after the second time I had to tap out and that was unusual for someone who likes to fuck all the time.

Now I'm sitting here listening to her talk about not being with me. She must've lost her damn mind if the thought even

crossed her mind about being with another. I had to remind her

that she's fucking with a boss and what I say goes. Yup I had

her ass hollering all night.

"Hey baby." She said when she opened her eyes.

"Hey sexy." I kissed her lips and waited for her to come

out the bathroom. She hated talking to me with morning breath.

I don't blame her but I wouldn't hold it against her either.

"Where are you going?" I asked watching her put

clothes on.

"I have to get your daughter."

"Nah. I already talked to your mom. We're spending the

day together. Get dressed and meet me downstairs." I left her

in the room and called Gage and Khalid and told them I would

be unreachable. I made plans to have her pampered all day.

She pushed my daughter out and even though I don't believe in

push gifts she still deserved everything. We were eating at one

of the expensive ass restaurants and I had everything set up so I

could propose to her but that was cut short when the bitch

walked in and came straight for us.

"Well don't you too look comfy?" My ex Shana said and sat down next to me. Melina didn't say anything nor did she give me a reaction to go off of.

"Excuse me but who are you?"

"I'm your new best friend." Shana said with a smirk on her face.

"Do we have the same dad?" I knew exactly where Melina was going with it.

"Ugh, no."

"Exactly. See my sisters are the only best friends I have. Unless you came from my dads' nutsack you and I will never be that. And before you ask no we're not taking applications." I couldn't hold my laugh in and did it right it Shana's face.

"Oh you think its funny Bruno? Let's see how funny it is six months from now." My entire expression changed. Here I was getting ready to propose and this bitch start talking that nonsense. Melina sat there cutting her steak like it wasn't bothering her.

"What do you want him to do? Shana is it?" Melina asked her sticking the steak in her mouth.

"Mmmmm Bruno this steak is so good. It's to die for just like you said my pussy was." She smirked and I spit my soda out.

"You told her that?"

"Yup. You see Shana you coming here didn't throw a monkey wrench in anything he and I have together. You can have this so called kid by him and what I have in between my legs will still have him come back. Ain't that right baby." She said reaching over and kissing my lips.

"I ain't never leaving you alone Melina. Shana whatever it is you're trying to do ain't working. If and it's a strong if that's my baby I will take care of it but trust and believe you won't get a dime from me before a test is done. Oh and don't even think about trying to schedule someone else to swab the baby. I'm hipped to tricks paying people off to change the results." She rolled her eyes and went to stand. I could see how mad she was.

"This ain't over Bruno."

"Oh but it is. That man right there belongs to me and only me. If you have a problem with him then we can go

198

outside and handle it like two adults. Otherwise, don't contact him until that baby is born." Melina mushed her in the forehead so hard she fell into the waiter.

"I will squeeze the life out of you in front of all these people if you even think about laying hands on my girl."

"I told you baby girl. What I have right here has him head over heels?" Shana stormed out the place and I put my head down shaking it. Melina was a mess and she knew it. Out of all three sisters she had to be the toughest. I'm not saying the other two couldn't hold their own but they were a little less violent.

"Damn baby. You weren't playing any games huh?"

"Do you like the way I fuck the shit out of you? Or how I make that dick cum so hard you need time to recuperate?"

"You know I do."

"Then hell no I'm not playing games when it comes to you. If I can't be with anyone else neither will you. If that means I have to shoot a bitch you already know I don't have a problem with it."

"Damn I think you just made my dick hard. Come give

me a kiss." She pushed her seat back and came to sit on my lap.

I let my hand go up and her shirt and for a minute we forgot

where we were until the manager cleared his throat and asked

if I was ready. I nodded my head and had her sit back down. I

saw him walking up and I knew she would lose it when she

saw him. She was a huge fan of his. I heard the music playing

on the intercom.

"Baby, this is my song." She started bopping her head.

He started singing and her head snapped.

"Wait, is that Ginuwine?" Melina asked me.

"Hold on. Is he singing to me?" When he stopped in

front of her she almost lost it. She sung the words with him and

grinded a little in her seat.

As the day goes by I'm always thinking of your face.

Your hair, your eyes, your sweet lips and the way they taste,

you got me going on a high that I have never felt, a beautiful

thing, This thing we got is so amazing, it's what I love the most,

it's how we can talk and how we laugh, the fact of how we're

so close, it's no illusion, but its magic, no tricks involved, in

you I got it all. I'm in love, I'm in love, do you hear me, was so scared, was not prepared. I'm so in love.

He sung the hell out of the song and he just ought of for the amount of money I paid to get him to do it. It was well worth it when I saw her face. I saw people standing taking photos and a few seconds later the entire restaurant was singing along with him. As the song went off I got down on one knee in front of her. I opened the box and the seven carat yellow diamond I got for her blinded everyone in there. She covered her mouth.

"Melina, I want to start off by saying I never thought in a million years I would find a woman to get me on one knee. You came into my life and a nigga has been on a high that I can't come down from. Yes, I made some mistakes but through it all we found our way back to one another. There's not another woman out there that can make me feel the way you do. Melina you and my daughter are my life and there's nothing in this world left for me to do except make you my wife. Will you marry me?" She nodded her head yes and I slid the ring on her finger. You could hear all the ladies screaming in the background. Ginuwine congratulated me and ended up staying to eat and take pictures.

"I love you Melina Woods. Well it will be Melina Jackson soon."

"I love you too Bruno Jackson and I can't wait to be your wife." I paid for our food and went home to make love to my new fiancé.

Maci

I could watch Bruno's proposal over and over to my sister Melina. Somebody taped it and posted it online. I'm not saying the one I got wasn't good but damn this nigga had Ginuwine come and sing to her. I may be young but I will ride that pony anytime. I don't even care that I'm a newbie to the sex game that man can have his way with me. Khalid came in and asked me if I was jealous I told him no. I don't ever want him to feel that way. I may talk shit about Ginuwine but he doesn't have shit on my man.

We all were going to Gage's and Meadows house for a small party. Now that all of us were engaged to three boss ass niggas my parents wanted to celebrate. We could've had it at their house but my dad said he wanted to fuck my mom into a coma later and he didn't want to wait for everyone to leave. Yup he said it just like that. My parents were strung out on each other. Bruno's parents were coming for a little but then they were taking Morgan with them. Of course her father wasn't too happy with that but Melina told him to get over it. It's not like she was going with a stranger.

"Baby are you going to be acting the same way with our kid?" I asked Khalid as we were getting dressed for the barbeque."

"Probably. Look how I am with you and you're not a baby."

"Yea, I guess."

"Maci, come here real quick." The way he said it had me nervous. I ran in the bedroom and this nigga was stroking his dick.

"Really Khalid. I thought something was wrong."

"It is. My dick is hard and the only way it can go down is if you suck on it."

"Hmmm. Suck on it. You sure you don't want me to sit on it?" I asked already licking up and down on it and sucking on the tip.

"Shit baby. I'll let you know after you finish drinking."
His hand was on my head and he was watching me. He
enjoyed doing that. Not too long after I tasted his juice that was
spitting out and swallowed all of it.

"Bend that ass over." I turned around and did what he
said. His lips were sucking my clit so good I came right away.
I felt him put his fingers in my ass and pussy and fuck me with
them. We never had anal sex but this right here had me
wanting to try it. I threw my ass back a little while he did it and
let my juices rush out.

"Yea, Maci. That's what I'm talking about." He licked
all of it up.

"I see my friend is awake."

"He is. So what are you going to do about it?"

"Nothing. He doesn't want to feel in me." He grabbed
me back by the waist and slammed me down on it.

"Ahhh shit Khalid. I am about to cum already." He
turned me over and fucked me so good I didn't even want to
attend the party anymore. All I wanted to do was sleep. He
must've fallen asleep with me because both of our phones were

ringing off the hook asking where we were. I woke him up and we took a quick shower together and rushed over there.

"Damn baby. We can have sex anymore before we go out."

"Why not?"

"Because we put each other to sleep."

"That's how you know we belong together."

"Without a doubt baby." We got out and went inside to find everyone else. The party was popping but I felt like more and more people were coming. That was odd being though Gage didn't want too many people to know where he lived; especially being though he could find his brother's crazy ass.

"Khalid, what is Maribel doing here?" I pointed to her and he looked more confused than I did.

"I don't know. What the hell is going on? I know Gage didn't invite her so how she knows about it is beyond me. I went to stand up when I saw her coming towards us and he pulled me back down.

"I will knock her the fuck out if she says anything to you."

"Khalid."

"You are not about to lose my baby or be out here fighting." I nodded my head. It was no use arguing with him when he was right. I had a baby in my stomach and there was no need to be ratchet.

"Hello you two." She shocked both of us by speaking.

"What do you want?" Khalid said already angry she said hello.

"Nothing. I just wanted to say congratulations Khalid. I see you found one I couldn't get rid of."

"Nah, I wasn't that chick you could intimidate but I give you an A for effort."

"Touché." She lifted her glass and took a sip.

"Maribel, what are you doing here? How did you know about this?"

"What do you mean? There was a flyer and someone posted it all over Facebook." Khalid and I looked at each other.

"Can we see the post?" I didn't really care to speak to her more than usual but I needed some answers. We wanted to know who posted it. Khalid and I looked it over and didn't notice anything unusual about it until he said he noticed someone walk in that wasn't supposed to be there.

"FUCK! Go find your sisters and then come back to me."

"Khalid what's wrong?" He didn't answer and walked off.

"Oh shit." I heard Maribel yell out.

"What?"

"I can see why he ran off. Shit, is about to hit the fan."

"I wish someone tells me what is going on."

"It's Rylee."

"Who the fuck is Rylee?"

"Do you remember when I threw that drink in your face and we fought?"

"I remember beating your ass for it but yea." She gave me a fake smile.

"Well Rylee was the chick that your sister beat up."

"Ok, so why is she here?"

"Damn, you really don't know."

"No, now tell me." I yelled. I was getting pissed.

"Rylee, is my ex friend that used to fuck Gage."

"Oh that's it."

"Nah, we aren't friends anymore because she was crazy. Rylee, was obsessed over Gage and would do anything to make sure no other woman got him."

"What is that supposed to mean?"

"Look, I may not like you but if I were you I would be trying to find my sister before Rylee did. That bitch ain't wrapped too tight." She said and took another sip of her drink. I was about to walk off until I heard her say something that caught my attention.

"Damn, I haven't seen him in years." I glanced around to see who she was talking about and had no idea.

"Who?"

"Jesse." She said. *Jesse, Jesse.* I kept thinking in my head. I know that name.

"Jesse who."

"Gage's brother." The minute she said that my heart dropped. She pointed him out and I could already see the gun in his waist. He was looking around for someone and I bet it was my sister.

"Are you ok?" I could hear Maribel asking me but my head felt dizzy and my feet were stuck. My sister was in danger and I couldn't function. The room was spinning and before I could find a seat I felt my entire body hit the floor. My head bounced off it and it felt like something was gushing out.

"Somebody go find Khalid. NOW!" I heard Maribel scream and that was the last thing I heard.

Meadow

"Meadow cum for me baby." Gage was playing with my clit while I was on top riding the hell out of him.

"Yes Gage. Shittttt."

"I'm cumming too baby. Fuckkkkk." He grunted and released all he had in me. We talked about having more kids in the future and the way we practiced it would be happening sooner than later.

"I probably just got you pregnant." He laughed. I stood up and told him we had to hurry up and get back to the party. He and I ducked off an hour or so ago just to have sex. I'm sure people were downstairs looking for us. We took a shower and got dressed. We walked downstairs hand in hand and he introduced me to a lot of people. I started recognizing that the party had more people than I was comfortable with. It didn't matter because those were his people but it was weird to see so many when they weren't invited.

"Baby, who are all these people? Did you invite all of them?"

"No, but it's cool. Are you ok?"

"Yea. I just don't want anything to pop off."

"Ain't nobody that stupid."

"If you get uncomfortable tell me and I'll kick everyone the fuck out."

"Stop it. I'm fine."

We finished mingling when I felt the urge to pee. I wasn't using my downstairs bathrooms until the maid came the next day and bleached it. I'm sure with the amount of people here the bathroom was probably filthy. I stepped in the bedroom and went to the closet to take the test out I got from the store earlier today. I know Gage thinks he got me pregnant today but I believe he did the first day we got back together a month ago at my grand opening. I had the same symptoms as before. The back aches, vomiting, my breast was always sore and I couldn't take the dick like before.

I popped open both boxes. I was happy one of the tests had the hook like thing to it. It was a curve so the urine wouldn't touch you. I sat some tissue on the counter then wet both of them with my urine. I placed them on the sink when I came out and washed my hands while I waited for the results. I heard my bedroom door open and close and just assumed it was Gage but it was Melina.

"Oh shit bitch. What are you going to do if it's positive?"

"What do you mean what am I going to do? I'm keeping it duh?"

"I know that. I was saying are you going to tell him right away or wait like you did the last time?"

"No, I'm going to tell him right away. We are in a great space right now and I don't want to waste time arguing because I took my time telling him."

"Good. Now let's see if I'm going to be an auntie and if Morgan will have a cousin soon." She took my hand and we stepped inside together.

"I hope it's a boy." Melina said as I stood there crying and looking at the test. This was Gage's and I second chance at being parents and I was ecstatic. He was going to be so happy.

213

He still blames himself for what happened so hopefully this will cheer him up.

"Can you go get him for me Melina?" I asked. She gave me a hug and said she would send him up here. I wasn't in the mood to be down there anyway. I found a pair of pajamas to put on and went in the bathroom to change. I wasn't sure if he would come back in the room with anyone. I put my pajama pants on with a tank top and heard the bedroom door open. I heard the door lock and that was weird being though there were people downstairs.

"Come here baby. I have something that I think will make you happy." I heard the footsteps coming towards me and stood there with the biggest smile on my face. That smile turned into a frown when the person came into view. Fear instantly overtook my body and I used the bathroom on myself. I don't care what people say when you're scared to death you can have an accident. By no means am I a scary bitch but this man right here had me petrified.

"What, what are you doing here?" I was stuttering and trying to remain calm.

"Is that anyway to greet your new man?" This man was bugging.

"Jesse, you have to leave."

"Oh I am but you're coming with me." I tried to walk past him but he had a death grip on my arm.

"I see I'm about to be a father." He said looking down at the test on the sink.

"Jesse you and I never had sex."

"I know that but you're going to be my wife so I may as well start claiming it now." *Where the fuck is Gage? He should've been back up here by now.* I was able to get out his grip and run to the door but he snatched me back by the hair and told me if I didn't want to lose another baby I better do what he said.

"Get in the shower and clean yourself up. I'm not taking you anywhere smelling like piss." I wasn't even embarrassed that he said that. I didn't move and he pulled a gun out and pointed it at my stomach.

"Take them fucking clothes off and get in the shower. You have two minutes."

"Gage, is going to be up here Jesse and you know it's not going to end well for you."

"You don't have to worry about that. I have him covered downstairs." He threw his head back laughing. I turned the shower on and stepped inside and washed my body. He stood with his dick in his hands and jerking himself off. I jumped back when I saw his dick spitting cum out. I was more than disgusted. I stepped out while he was putting his dick back I and tried to throw some clothes on but he stopped me.

"Come here Meadow." I didn't move and he started yelling.

"Put your leg on my shoulder and let me eat that pussy the way my brother does. I want to see those sexy ass faces you make."

"Jesse please don't do this." His hand touched my leg to lift it but he stopped when his phone vibrated.

"Fuck. You're lucky we have to go. Throw those pants on and let's go." He snatched a hat out of Gage's closet and made me put it on. He opened the door and made me hold his hand go down in the crowd. It was as if no one saw anything wrong with what was going on because there was a commotion in the living room. He pushed me in the back seat of some car but the child locks were on and I couldn't get out. He sped out the driveway and thirty minutes later we parked in front of some house I never saw before.

"Get out." He yanked me out and opened the door to the house. He took me to the basement and locked the door. I heard his car leave. I tried to get out but the door was bolt locked and all the windows had boards over them. I searched the basement for hours to find anything to help me out and came up empty handed. I sat on the futon that was down there and turned the television on and laid there reflecting on my life. This was the exact reason I didn't want to deal with no thugs or as people call them a BOSS.

"This is Debra Eisenhower reporting live from Franklin Terrace where there has been reports of a shooting." I jumped up off the couch when I heard the woman say the name of my street. There were cops everywhere and I saw my house in the background. I waited for her to say someone was killed but she said it was breaking news and that the story was still developing. What is the fuck is going on?

Gage

Meadow and I had absolutely no business dipping off from the party like that knowing damn well we could've waited. Fuck it, she was about to be my wife so if she wanted it as her man I have to give it to her. I can't lie; a nigga was happy as hell she took me back. After I told her about my brother she did let me make love to her that night but she damn sure made me wait a week and a half to get anymore. She meant it when she told me I was in time out. I didn't mind as long as she was still in my life I could wait. Sex wasn't everything.

I had the same look of surprise on my face when we came out the room and all those people were standing there. The party was only supposed to consist of maybe forty people but it damn near looked to be almost two hundred. It made my girl feel uncomfortable but she claimed to be ok. When she told me that she was going to use the bathroom I started telling

218

people they had to go. It was after one in the morning anyway and they needed to go home.

"Yo, where's Meadow?" Khalid said when I saw him.

"She ran upstairs to use the bathroom why what's up?"

"Man, that crazy bitch Rylee here."

"WHAT?" That was the last person I needed to know where I lived or better yet even be in my house. He and I searched for her but it was so many people we couldn't find her.

"Hey, Meadow said she wants to see you in the room." Melina said and walked off into the other room. I was on my way out the kitchen when this dumb bitch pushed me into one of the bathrooms and stood there with a gun on me. I could've easily rushed her but what if the gun went off and caused a panic. I couldn't take the chance of something happening to people at my house.

"What Rylee?"

"Now why would you address me like that?"

"Rylee you got two minutes to tell me what you want and take that fucking gun off me." She lowered it just like I knew she would and started taking her clothes off. I can't from I was getting aroused watching her play with herself but I wasn't about to disrespect my girl or her house. I snatched her dumb ass up and told her to get dressed. She started spitting all this nonsense about being with me and some other shit but what caught me was her texting something or her cell phone and her telling me I had to wait a few more minutes.

"Wait for what? What type of game are you playing?"

"I'm not playing anything."

"Ok Rylee look. You have some good pussy and your head games are the bomb but two things. One your skills are no way better than my fiancé's and two you and I will never be together. Your obsession with me is sad and you need help. Why don't you go out there and hook up with one of the many men out there. I'm sure one of them will wife you up.

"I don't want them. I want you." She dropped to her knees and pulled my sweats down. I was able to keep my boxers up and pushed her back. I'm not sure if I would've been able to do that if she was able to wrap her lips around it. I heard something going on in the other room and pushed past

220

her. I opened the door and people were running to the living room and I heard some screaming. I pushed through the crowd and saw Maci lying on the ground and Melina was next to her.

"Where is Khalid?" She asked me and I looked around for him. I hit him on his phone and he answered and said he was in the bathroom. I told him he needed to get out here. I was on the phone with 911 when I heard him start bugging the fuck out. I saw people backing up and the look on their faces showed how scared they were.

"What happened to her?" He had Maribel yanked up by the shirt and she could barely speak from the way he was squeezing her throat. Bruno was able to get him off her right before the cops came in.

"I don't know Khalid. She asked me who was Rylee and I told her but then when I mentioned that I saw Jesse she looked like she saw a ghost a passed out."

"Who did you say she saw?" I was in her face making sure I wasn't bugging.

"Your brother. Jesse he was here." I backed up and went to run upstairs. I passed the EMT's with a stretcher. I was stopped dead in my tracks with Rylee pointing her gun at me again. People started screaming and the house was in pure chaos. I ran and heard a few shots. I didn't care about the burning sensations I was feeling. I had to find Meadow. I busted in the room and she was nowhere to be found. I ran in the bathroom and looked down at the sink and noticed the test.

"Is she in here?" I heard Bruno and Melina ask.

"No but she's pregnant. I have to find her." I ran down the steps and realized I was lightheaded. I found myself tumbling down the stairs and blacking out.

"Sir, can you hear me." I heard some guy asking and shining a light in my face.

"Yes, where am I?"

"We're still at your house. You've been shot twice in the stomach. We have to get you to a hospital." I didn't know how that was possible when she shot me from behind or did she? I don't even remember her shooting me. I could feel the cuff on my arm and a needle in the other.

"We're losing him."

"Bruno."

"I'm here bro. You're going to be fine."

"I don't care if I die. Please find Meadow and make sure her and the baby are safe."

"Gage, don't talk like that." I could hear Melina crying.

"Just do it." I heard the machines to the heart thing going off and that was it.

Jesse

Today was the best day of my life since getting out of jail. My brother was probably dead and I had both of my women with me. Yup. I had Rylee and Meadow. I know you're probably wondering what I'm doing with her but it's pretty funny. Rylee was the daughter of the woman I so called raped ten years ago.

You see I was sleeping with Rylee for a year before she and I came up with the plan to blackmail her mom. She and her mom never got along and hated one another with a passion. However, in order to get her mom to give her the inheritance her dad left when he died she had to get married per her mother. We decided that she should have her money now and not have to wait for it. Anyway, I would go in and sleep with her mom but other people would call it rape. I told her if she ever told I would release the tape I had on the Internet and as a corporate lawyer she couldn't do that. We explained what she had to do

224

in order for it not to be released and that was to change the clause for her inheritance.

A month later she did and Rylee got her money but I was obsessed with sleeping with her mom. It was like raping her was a hobby and she took it in every hole possible. Unfortunately, the bitch got smart and taped me and I got arrested and sent to jail for ten years thanks to my brother. That stupid nigga was supposed to get me off all the way but instead I spent ten years of my life behind bars. I know he's not a lawyer but his money was long and he should've done better. Rylee came to see me about two years ago and we came up with the plan to get my brother for all he had. But this crazy bitch became obsessed with Gage and fell in love.

By the time I came home he was involved with some chick named Meadow. I had no plans on fucking with her because I knew he was in love with her. However, the day I came to his house and she had that towel wrapped around her I was adamant about making her mine. The night I heard her and my brother fucking I tried my luck and opened the door. My brother had a soundproof room but the door was cracked. I

225

peeked in and home girl was sucking the hell out of his dick. Another night I came home and tried my luck again and the door was open. She was riding him this time and the faces she made turned me on so much I pulled my dick out and came in my hand. If Gage ever found out I did that my head would be served to my mother with no remorse.

My mom loved both of us and she was sour with him that I had to do that much time in jail too. That's why when I told her Meadow and I had a thing she was ok with making sure Gage didn't find out. The day at her house I asked her to make him leave and told her Meadow and I hadn't been able to spend time together and she made it happen. Even though my mom loved both of us she loved me more because I was the troubled child and could do no wrong in her eyes. She knew damn well I didn't have any business with my brothers' girl but she went right along with the shit.

"Damn, that was fun." Rylee said and dropped down to suck my dick. I don't know what my brother was thinking letting her go. She was the real deal when it came to sex.

"Suck all that shit out Rylee." When she was done I was ready to fuck but I didn't want her but I knew damn well I had to give Meadow some time to trust me before she gave it up. She was pregnant too. I know that it was about to have a niggas head gone.

"Tell me what happened?"

"Shit is fucked up over there."

"What you mean?"

"Something happened to Khalid's girl that she had to be put on a stretcher and taken to the hospital. I shot your brother twice in the stomach and you have his bitch. What else could we possibly need?"

"Is he dead?"

"I think so. He was talking to Bruno and flat lined."

"How did you get away?"

"After I shot him I ran in the bathroom. No one knew it was me because everyone was running in different directions. I waited five minutes and pretended I was using the bathroom. I sat back and watched it all then slipped out the back door. Look, the shit made the news." She turned the television up

227

and we listened to her say there was a shooting and the person was still on the loose.

"What do you want to do about her?"

"After I fuck her a few times you can kill her."

"Why do you want to fuck her? You better not be in love with her?"

"Cut the shit Rylee. You're in love with my brother."

"That was before. Since you've been home it's been all about you."

"You telling me you didn't try and sleep with him tonight?"

"It was for old times' sake."

"Exactly. Get you petty ass over here so I can fuck you in the ass. I haven't done that with anyone since I left jail."

"I bet there ass didn't feel as good as mine though."

"You're right. I didn't have a pussy to play with and I damn sure wasn't touching a dick." Say what you want but if you can fuck a bitch in the ass you can do a man too and ten years will make a nigga say fuck it.

"Let's go check on this bitch." I said to Rylee when we were done. I unlocked the locks and opened the basement door.

"WHERE THE FUCK IS SHE?"

Made in United States
Orlando, FL
13 August 2022

20971629R00138